SAVING THE STAR

Rachel Bowdler

CONTENT WARNINGS

Blood, violence, death, and strong language

References to war, poverty, and assault

References to drink and drugs

PROLOGUE

Atlanta Stone should have stayed at the party. She knew that as soon as she stumbled up the steps to her hotel suite, her sharp stilettos snagging in the cream carpet, all while cursing the fact that the elevator had been out of service in a string of drunken slurs coherent only to her.

"S'pposed t' be five-star hotel, f' God's sake. Fuckin' mess."

She wasn't talking about the hotel anymore. *She* was the mess. She didn't care. She had been a mess for a long time now. *The* mess, really, if she were matched up against the rest of her family, which she often was. Her brother was the squeaky-clean angel. Her mother was the silver-screen goddess. Her stepfather was the charitable philanthropist. Atlanta was the mess.

She liked it that way.

Her family, not so much. They certainly wouldn't be happy that she was coming in at four o'clock in the morning intoxicated again, cheeks pink from the London frost that had very nearly bitten off one of her toes on the walk back. She would never get used to the British winter. The sooner she got back to sunny LA, the better.

Inside, though, tequila still warmed her veins more than enough to make up for it, dulling her senses. It was why, when she finally reached her floor eight stories up, her heels now dangling from her hands instead of on her tender feet, she thought nothing of the fact that her mother's door — the one she had strategically taken beside Atlanta's own room — had swung open and creaked on its hinges. She thought nothing of the sudden shuffling and shouting coming from within, thinking that perhaps her family were awake because of jet lag or had found out that Atlanta had snuck out again and were waiting for her to get home.

Worry tore through her only when the gunshot sounded, the explosion thrusting a sharp dagger of clarity through Atlanta's drug-mottled haze.

She flinched at the sound and dropped her shoes and purse to the floor. "Mom?" she called, stumbling straight past her own door and into her mother's room.

With only a mere glimpse, she saw it was a mess. The glass doors leading to the balcony were splattered with crimson, and every vase, every lampshade, and every sad little sachet of English-breakfast tea were upturned and strewn around the place.

The breath was forced out of Atlanta as a broad shoulder sent her tumbling to the floor. Her head hit the wall with a sickening crunch, and yet somehow, she found it in herself to pry her eyelids open again against the searing, white-hot agony. Her vision swam, from both the drink and drugs and the bang to the head. Still, the cold, granite eyes of her attacker pierced into her, clear as day. Trepidation flickered in those stone eyes, as though *she* had caught *him* off guard. Trepidation and loathing, and something far darker.

He wanted to hurt her.

His hood slipped from his head as he scowled down at her sorry state splayed across the floor, revealing the salt-and-pepper buzz cut of a middle-aged man. It was his mouth she would remember when everything else faded to black, though, twisted into an ugly sneer and bracketed with deep-etched lines.

Atlanta scrambled backward, past fallen paintings and thorned rose stems, when she saw what he held, what he was lifting to her head. A gun, black and glinting against the light of the hallway's chandeliers. "No. No," she pleaded, voice a feeble rasp. "No. Please. Please don't."

His finger twitched on the trigger. She felt the blood leach from her face at the knowledge that this would be the end of her. She would die alone, in a hotel room, drugs and alcohol still pumping through her system and the sour taste of a stranger's kiss on her lips. She had not even the luxury of a clear mind before she went.

Where was her mother? Where was Weston? Oh God, where was Anderson?

Her heart stuttered with panic, so erratically that she thought — *hoped* — he would not have to put a bullet through it to kill her. Her own body would get there first, send her into cardiac arrest. It wasn't unheard of with the amount of shit she had taken tonight.

She should have screamed. She hadn't even screamed yet. She opened her mouth, about to let what would be perhaps her last breath rip through the world.

"They're here," a low voice snarled before she could part with her shriek. It didn't come from the man holding the gun to her head. *There was more than one of them.* Atlanta's terror intensified threefold. "We need to go. *Now.*"

The gunman swore. Atlanta used the distraction to her advantage, swinging her legs beneath his feet before stumbling up onto her own and making a run for the en suite bathroom to her left. She looked back over her shoulder only once, and saw that he was doing the same. His panicked gaze melded into a determined grit that slithered from him and across the floor and seeped into Atlanta's skin and bones like ice.

Silent sobs racked her body when she finally bolted herself in the bathroom. A sticky warmth trickled down her neck, and darkness teetered on the edge of her vision. Her lungs tightened with lack of air as she listened desperately, waiting for the thud of their footsteps to return for her, to finish her off.

Instead, the slam of a door rang out, and

then... nothing.

No sound. No gunshots. No death.

Only Atlanta, slumped in darkness until darkness became her.

ONE

Beck Harris's upper lip curled into an instinctive sneer of disgust as she parked by the water fountain in the center of the Stones' driveway — a fucking *water fountain*. She was used to wealth and grandeur by now, but being exposed to it in her work life hadn't done anything to quell the scorn that clawed through her every time she rolled up to her next assignment.

And this... this was excessive, even up against the usual billionaire CEOs or arrogant politicians who hired her.

This was a joke.

The stately home loomed before the English countryside like a castle, casting everything in elongated, pointy shadows. Ivy, half-killed off from the bitter winter they were having, crawled up the old stone walls toward the turrets, and the windows were so big that it must have cost an arm and a leg just to buy curtains large enough to hang over them. Beside Beck's own black SUV and the two identical cars belonging to her colleagues, a white Lamborghini and a flame-red Ferrari rested side by side, polished enough that Beck could see the distorted reflection of her own car in the bright paint.

Her sympathy for the Stone family dwindled by the minute as she worked up the resolve to finally get out of the car and toss herself to the wolves. It was no wonder they were robbed, with their wealth flaunted for anyone to see. They could clearly afford to lose a few valuables.

An elegant middle-aged woman emerged from the arched threshold of the manor to greet Beck. Though she had neither the time nor the patience to keep up with celebrities, she recognized Minerva Stone immediately from the films she'd watched with her brother as a child. The actress had been blonde and young, then: now, her dark hair was plastered to her scalp in a high ponytail, and her face was beginning to crease here and there. Still, her golden skin remained taut over regal cheekbones, highlighting the life of luxury she had lived — and probably the many facelifts that came with it.

Beck did not deign to take off her sunglasses as she nodded her greeting, slamming the car door and locking it with finality.

"You must be Beck Harris." Minerva's American accent grated like nails on a chalkboard, and Beck tried to tune it out.

"Correct." Beck nodded, waving when she noticed their security detail, Phil, lingering just behind Minerva with his arms crossed over his puffed chest. He offered a wary bob of his bald head in return, his lips pursed into a thin line. Clearly,

Beck wasn't the only one unhappy with her assignment, though Phil had worked for the Stones for far longer than her. "And you're Minerva Stone."

"In the flesh." Minerva threw her arms out as though she were modeling on a catwalk. "I assume you've been briefed on our… situation."

"Armed robbery," Beck rattled off calmly as they ambled across the gravel. "Two gunmen, after a necklace your husband had just bought in an auction, but they didn't find it because it was locked up in a safe somewhere off the property. You were asleep, he wasn't. They shot him in the leg before he could fight back. Your daughter came in at the sound of the gunfire and saw one of the shooters' faces before they left. Have I missed anything?"

Minerva faltered for only a moment, glancing at Beck sidelong with something she had learned not to take personally: surprise. It still irritated her to no end that her clients expected less of her, particularly because she knew that Phil and her other male colleagues wouldn't have received the same regard, but she pushed it down and kept her chin high.

"No, Miss Harris, I think that sums it up quite well."

"Good." Beck flashed a terse smile as Minerva led her into the manor. It was even more lavish inside, with a chandelier greeting them in the open hallway and a spiral staircase winding to the second floor. Beck fought the urge to wipe her feet on the welcome mat as she examined the array of paintings hung on the wall. If she hadn't known any better, she would have sworn the place was a museum rather than a holiday estate.

"I'm sure you were made aware that this is not our permanent residence. We rented the place out after the robbery while my husband, Weston, finishes off his work in London. Next week we'll be flying back to LA."

Finally Beck slid her sunglasses off to meet Minerva's gaze. The actress's eyes were a piercing blue, red-rimmed and weary. The vulnerability they bore made Beck forget for a moment that she was a world-famous celebrity. If not for the sophisticated dress and dewy skin, Minerva could have been any other woman who needed help. "That's not a problem, Mrs. Stone."

"There's something else I wished to ask of you." Minerva's heels clicked against the marble floor as she continued down a narrow hallway lined by brass sconces. It brought them out into a large kitchen with clinically white walls that were blindingly bright, bathed as they were in sunlight. The marble countertops were spotless — whether from a maid or because the Stone family didn't cook, Beck couldn't guess. Beyond the closed patio doors, yards and yards of artificially green grass yawned out before them. A round-bellied man in khaki pants hunched over a golf putt not too far from the wooden terrace, preparing to swing the club. Bandages covered his left calf, and he moved cautiously on his feet. Weston Wilder, Minerva's husband. He had been the only one seriously injured in the attack, but the bullet wound had been superficial enough that he'd only needed a week or so in the hospital. Another man, slim and golden-haired, leaned against his own club with his back to them. Anderson Stone, Minerva's son, if Beck had to guess.

Beck snapped her attention away when she realized that she hadn't replied yet. "Please, go on."

Minerva rested against the counter, her false nails, pointed and red, tracing spirals into the surface. "I read your file. You certainly have plenty of experience for such a young woman."

Beck's eyes narrowed. Minerva was lucky she had put "young" in front of that, though at thirty Beck didn't feel worthy of the title anymore. It was true, though, that she had experience. She had joined the military at eighteen and started out as a close protection officer five years later. She had dealt with all manner of things by now, so much so that she didn't think much else could surprise her. "Thank you, Mrs. Stone."

"You came with a glowing recommendation. With that in mind, I was wondering if perhaps you might use some of your company's resources to carry out your own investigation."

"An investigation?" Beck questioned, brows drawing together.

"The people who attacked my family are still out there, Miss Harris, and my daughter has seen at least one of their faces. I'd like you to bring them to justice."

"I'm a protection officer, Mrs. Stone. Not a detective."

"I understand that," Minerva said coolly, "and yet you and I both know the police won't do enough to keep us safe, certainly not when we'll be out of the country soon. I'm not asking for you to work day and night on this, but it would bring me a certain comfort to know that you are looking for the criminals, too, when you aren't taking care of my daughter."

Reluctantly, Beck sighed in agreement. "I'll see what I can do."

"Thank you, Miss Harris." Minerva smiled pleasantly before pulling out two glasses from the overhead cupboard. Beck expected her to fill them at the tap, but instead she pulled a jug with a filter from the fridge and poured the water from that. *Rich people*, Beck scoffed internally, but accepted the drink when it was offered nonetheless. It tasted no different, either way.

"Atlanta is a late riser, so it'll be a few hours before I can properly introduce you to her. I emailed over her work schedule for the next few weeks, and I'll be sure to have her assistant in LA keep it updated for you. I'd like to apologize in advance. My daughter can be quite..." Minerva winced as she searched for the apt word, before settling on "difficult."

Beck stopped sipping on her fancy water to

deepen her frown. "I was under the impression that your daughter was an adult, Mrs. Stone."

"Oh, she is." Minerva waved a dismissive hand. "But she started her rebellious phase at sixteen and never quite came back out of it. I'm sure you've seen the news articles and whatnot."

Beck hadn't, but she could only imagine what it was that twenty-something celebrities got up to these days. What on earth was she walking into here?

Despite the dread wriggling through her gut, Beck forced her most polite smile and set her glass down. "I'm sure we'll be just fine."

❋ ❋ ❋

Atlanta rose just after midday — a habit she would be sorry to break when her work schedule started up again next week — to find a woman clad in all back standing with a rigid posture in her kitchen. She raised an eyebrow and brushed past her carelessly to make herself some coffee.

"I thought the audition for *Women in Black* wasn't until next week."

If the woman understood the joke, she didn't show it. Atlanta rounded the breakfast bar again, scrutinizing her. She couldn't have been that much older than her brother — twenty-seven, twenty-eight at most — but an air of maturity rolled from her that even her mother didn't quite possess yet. Her straight dark hair was tied into a low ponytail, her face bare of much makeup. Though she was pretty — gorgeous, actually — with an olive skin tone and sharp jaw, she was dressed too plainly to be one of her brother's conquests. Much too plainly.

She stared at Atlanta so blankly that Atlanta wondered if her stepfather, Weston, had purchased a waxwork from Madame Tussauds without telling her. She wouldn't put it past him. Not after he had bought a life-sized stuffed elephant to keep in his hallway last year. To check, she waved a hand in front of the woman's face. The woman didn't so much as blink, though her hazel eyes narrowed on Atlanta. "Can I help you, Miss Stone?"

"Are you another detective?" Her obvious ability to move and speak set Atlanta's suspicions at ease, and she returned to the boiling kettle and the instant — awful — coffee grains in her mug. "I've already told them everything I know."

"No. I work for the World Protection Group. I'm your new close protection officer."

After becoming bored enough to watch a few of the British soap operas on television over the past few days, Atlanta recognized the woman's broad accent to sound quite like the ones she'd heard on *Coronation Street*, with a thick lilt and soft, lazy vowels. Northern, then. The way it mingled with her gravelly tone wasn't altogether unpleasant, and Atlanta couldn't help but let an indulgent smirk curl at her lips.

She heaped a tooth-rotting amount of sugar

into her coffee before throwing the spoon into the basin with a clatter. "And what's that in English?"

"I suppose to people like you, it's a body-guard."

Atlanta did not miss the way "people like you" was said, as though she were beneath her. She scowled and crossed her arms over her chest, well aware of the fact that the position exposed a dangerous amount of cleavage, with only her satin nightgown protecting her bare body. She didn't care enough to cover up with her robe. "A body-guard?"

"Yes, miss." The woman cast her a stand-offish glance, all downturned, plump lips and clenched, square jaw. If she could have looked down her nose at Atlanta, she probably would have, but they were near enough the same height. The observation caused Atlanta to bite back a laugh of disbelief. How the hell was this woman supposed to protect her? "Your mother hired me to monitor your safety until further notice."

"Oh, did she?" Atlanta retorted, annoyance fringing her words.

"Is that a problem, miss?" She arched her eyebrow as though baiting Atlanta.

Atlanta gritted her teeth. "Stop calling me 'miss.'"

"How should I address you, then, miss?" The corner of her mouth twitched up proudly. Atlanta tried not to notice how attractive her arrogance made her. It was a weakness: one she was trying to get over after her last so-called relationship.

"Don't," Atlanta replied bluntly. "You won't need to address me. I'll have you let go before the end of the day. *Un*dressing me, on the other hand, I might allow."

The woman opened her mouth to reply, but the sound of stilettos against tile stopped them both in their tracks. Minerva entered the kitchen with a nonchalance that never failed to shock Atlanta, hooking a pair of diamond-studded earrings through her lobes and humming an old song from the only album — thank god — that she had ever released. Needless to say, it had never made it to the top ten and Minerva returned to her acting career not long after.

She stopped when she noticed Atlanta. "Oh, good, you're up. And I see you've met Beck."

"Beck the bodyguard," Atlanta remarked. "You can stop wasting her time now, Mother. I don't need a babysitter."

"I beg to differ," Minerva said.

At the same time, Beck said shortly, "I'm not a babysitter."

"This is ridiculous." Atlanta scoffed and took a sip of her coffee, fighting the urge to wince against the bitter aftertaste.

Minerva rounded the counter and patted Atlanta on the shoulder before stealing her coffee. Her red lipstick stained the rim of the mug as she took a swig, and Atlanta glared. "Don't waste your breath fighting me on this, all right? Your stepfather was shot and you nearly were, too. You could do with the extra security."

A sneer uncoiled on Atlanta's features, though it was forced. She didn't need reminding of that night and what had almost come of it. The dark barrel of the gun pointed between her eyes still haunted her. "I had a minor concussion. I was fine."

"Until we feel safe again, Beck and her colleagues will be here with us."

"And how is average-height, average-build Beck going to protect me if Mr. Armed Robber decides to come back for us? *Your* bodyguard is twice the size of you. Mine probably couldn't reach the cereal shelf in Waitrose."

Beck cleared her throat, nudging her jacket away from her hip just slightly to reveal a glimpse of a handgun tucked away in her holster.

"Congratulations. You own the same weapon as fifty percent of Americans — including my mother."

"Miss Harris is one of the best officers in the company," Minerva argued, shooting Atlanta a warning glance that had stopped having any effect on her about ten years ago.

"I can assure you you're in safe hands, Miss Stone," Beck added. "Believe me, I'm handy with more than just a gun. My company only hires the best."

"Whatever." Atlanta rolled her eyes, already walking away. It was too early for this, and she was not nearly drunk enough. "As long as it's coming out of your paycheck, Mom."

"Oh, Atlanta, stop being so difficult," Minerva huffed from the kitchen. Atlanta only rolled her eyes again and went back to bed.

TWO

When Beck had first gotten this job, just out of the military, she would have expected it to involve something much more exciting than watching a bleach-blonde rich girl meditating and performing yoga in the back garden. She swallowed down her sigh, her hands crossed behind her back, and kicked up the artificial grass with the steel toe cap of her boot.

It was freezing out, Atlanta's breath curling around her as she pressed her palms together and took a few drawn-out breaths, eyes closed tightly. Beck was certain the woman was doing this just to taunt her and pursed her lips together, unamused, as she scoured the acres of land for any sign of danger. Nothing. According to Minerva, nobody knew that the family had rented this home in the British countryside. Why Beck couldn't have just met them in London tomorrow, then, she had no idea.

Atlanta squinted open one eye as she balanced on her right foot and lifted the other to her knee. "You're welcome to join in, Miss Harris."

"I'm quite all right, thanks." Beck feigned politeness as best she could.

"I bet you are." Atlanta bent over into down-ward-dog position so that her rear end was on full display, with only a thin pair of yoga pants preserving her modesty. Beck pretended not to notice the visible lines of her underwear, or the fact that it was clear from her rounded muscles that Atlanta kept herself in good shape. She pretended not to notice the flirtatious edge to her tone, either. This must be how Atlanta Stone got her way with everybody, and Beck wasn't stupid enough to humor her — even if she was irritatingly perfect to look at. "Enjoying the view?"

Beck kept her features devoid of any reaction as her attention slid past Atlanta, to the far end of the lawn. "I've seen better, miss."

Atlanta scoffed and straightened, her cheeks flushed from the blood rushing to her head. "Don't you have anything better to do than hover around me like a fly?"

"I can think of a million things, love," Beck replied sharply. "Believe me."

"Don't let me stop you."

Beck ignored her, glowering at nothing in particular. It didn't stop Atlanta from continuing on.

"Aren't you a little too young to play this Kevin Costner–type thing?"

"I've never heard that one before," Beck deadpanned sarcastically. Atlanta was not the first — and no doubt would not be the last — to compare her to Whitney Houston's love interest in *The Bodyguard*. Beck had not even seen the movie, nor did she have any desire to. "I'm not *playing* anything. This is my job."

Atlanta shrugged, smirking as she rolled up her yoga mat, bare toes wiggling in the plastic blades of grass. "I'm just saying. I suppose you *are* a little more attractive than him. I'll give you that."

"Hmm," Beck hummed under her breath, placing her hands in her pockets as the cold began to bite at them. "I've heard that before, too."

"And yet you've kept so modest, I see." Atlanta's chocolate-brown eyes danced as she looked up at Beck properly for the first time since this morning, gathering her yoga mat beneath her arm. They had been a shock, those eyes: so dark while the rest of her was made of light, and so unlike her mother's.

"And I suppose you'd know a lot about modesty yourself, Miss Stone," Beck retorted, eyeing the woman's false nails and the dark hair beginning to uproot beneath the peroxide with more than a little judgment. Still, she had seen people far falser than Atlanta and her mother in her time. Her golden skin seemed to be sun-kissed rather than sprayed on, and she wore no makeup today.

None of that changed her terrible attitude, though. Beck was already tired of her. The sooner this was over, the better.

"What are you implying, Miss Harris?"

Beck sought to change the subject quickly. "Your mother asked me to look into the robbery while I'm here. I've been briefed, of course, but if you'd be willing to write a report when you've time, that would help speed things up. I believe you talked to a forensic artist?"

Atlanta's face darkened as she stood up, and for the first time, Beck caught a glimpse of what lived beneath that cocky façade. She was not invincible — it was clear that learning so in that posh hotel she'd been staying in had knocked the wind from her. "I tried," she said finally. Beck did not miss the ragged breath that fell with her words. "The guy was an average Joe, no distinct features. We couldn't get much."

"Still," Beck said, "write them down for me, and I'll see if I can dig anything up on our database."

"Aren't I supposed to be telling *you* what to do?" Atlanta's brows lifted in accusation.

"You're not my employer, Miss Stone," Beck replied dryly. "Your mother is. You can help me with this or you can not help me. The sooner you let me do my job, though, the sooner I can find your attackers and we can stop this little charade."

"And why would one affect the other? I'm famous. I'm already in danger all the time."

Beck narrowed her eyes. Was the girl really that clueless? "You saw his face. You're the only one who knows what one of them looks like, who can identify him. That might very well make you his next target, love. As long as that's the case, you're in more danger than you've ever been in before."

The color drained from Atlanta's face until Beck wondered if she was going to pass out on her. So she really hadn't thought of that, had been naive enough to think herself safe again, just like that. Beck didn't know whether to pity the woman or judge her for it.

"You think he'd come back for me?" The words were whispered and shaky: a glimpse into who she was when she wasn't pretending.

Beck shrugged. "Who knows? It's different when you're in the public eye. He can't be reckless again and get caught, not when you're constantly surrounded by people. That makes you difficult to get to. There's every chance he might save himself the hassle, especially if he's working with an organization."

That seemed to soothe her slightly, though Beck hadn't particularly intended it to. Atlanta relaxed her shoulders, swallowing down her fear.

"Still," Beck added nonchalantly, "better safe than sorry, don't you think, Miss Stone?"

"I'll write you the report," Atlanta agreed. "I'll have it to you by tomorrow."

"Good."

The blond-haired man that Beck had seen golfing earlier emerged from the patio doors, and skipped the steps down onto the grass two at a time. Beck watched him carefully, scrutinizing him as he approached. He was youthful, but the faint crow's feet creasing the corners of his eyes said he was older than he appeared, just like Minerva. Where Atlanta's hair was clearly dyed for her to achieve the golden tone, his seemed natural, styled carefully. Their eyes, though, were the same, and he could not have been mistaken as anybody other than her brother.

He ignored Beck's presence completely, his focus falling straight to Atlanta. "I see you've got a new bodyguard, too."

Eric had been assigned to Anderson Stone, Atlanta's brother, at the same time Beck had been tasked with Atlanta, though she hadn't seen him yet. She searched behind the tall man but spotted no one. His first day, and he was already slacking.

"And an extremely pleasant one at that." Atlanta shot Beck a look that she pretended not to notice. Instead she held out her hand.

"I'm Beck Harris."

"Anderson," he replied with little interest. He shook her hand only once before it fell back to his side. Beck already liked him even less than the rest of the family.

"Why don't you take a break, Miss Harris?" Atlanta suggested, hope swelling in her tone. "I don't plan on leaving this place today, so you might as well stalk me from the security cameras instead."

Beck had been told about the security office at the side of the house. She hoped to god that Eric or Phil was there so that she would have somebody other than stuck-up celebrities to talk to today. "All right. You have my number in your phone."

"That's very forward of you."

Beck forced herself not to roll her eyes. Would the woman ever stop trying to get a rise out of her? "Call if you need anything."

"Oh, I won't," Atlanta drawled sweetly. "Namaste."

Beck only nodded at Anderson in goodbye and left in search of her new office.

She had not even completed her first day, and she was already over it.

* * *

The office was snug, and Beck would have much rather spent the rest of her day here than follow Atlanta around while she did yoga and painted her nails. Phil sat at the computer across from her, one eye on the security cameras and the other on the football game playing on his phone. Beck would have chided him for it, only it was clear no threat lived in this area aside from perhaps a few deer, and no armed robber would be stupid enough to try to penetrate the wrought-iron gates and security systems at the front of the manor.

Instead she skimmed over the files that had been emailed over to her earlier surrounding the attack on the Stones.

"You were on duty the night of the attack, right?" she murmured, voice low in concentration as she shuffled through the papers.

"Yep." Phil flashed her a look of annoyance

as he paused the game and put his phone down. He was much more the standard bodyguard type than Beck, with stubble casting a rough edge across his features and a cockney accent making him sound gruff. "We were let off at around eleven, when they got home from a charity ball. The hotel was supposed to be secure for folk like them. A few of our men —"

Beck's barbed glare soon cut him off.

"Sorry... *people*," he corrected wryly, "work there through the week, since the hotel needs the extra security with all the rich and famous who stay there."

"But that night, two armed robbers managed to just walk in." Beck's brows knitted together, and she pinched the bridge of her nose in an attempt to understand. "None of ours were working that night?"

"Apparently not." Eric shrugged, running his chubby fingers across his smooth scalp as though it was just as much a mystery to him.

"And the security footage was accidentally wiped." It wasn't a question. She had already triple-checked the fact and found nothing.

"So they say."

"It's awfully convenient, isn't it?"

Eric pursed his lips together in agreement. "What are you thinking?"

Beck sighed and slid the files away before they overwhelmed her. "I'm thinking that somebody out there knows what happened that night.

Somebody in that hotel must have seen something."

"They questioned everybody they could find, Beck. They got nothing."

Beck bit down on her lip and returned her focus to the computer screen, where the live feed of the manor's CCTV footage flickered in black and white. Atlanta was in her bedroom, Anderson and Minerva in the kitchen, and Wes in his study. It was like a bloody game of Cluedo.

Her attention zeroed in on Atlanta, who wouldn't have been visible from the hallway's security camera were her door not cracked open — intentionally, probably, if she knew Beck could see. Her figure barely stirred save for her fingers, typing furiously across her bright phone screen.

She might be safe here, but how long would it last?

"Maybe they just haven't been asking the right questions."

THREE

Atlanta couldn't say exactly why she had decided to climb down the drainpipe from her balcony rather than leave through the front door. Her new bodyguard hadn't shown her face for hours, and her mother had taken an early night with Weston. Perhaps she was making up for an adolescence lost to flashing lights and long hours spent in television studios. Or perhaps she was just bored.

Perhaps just a little bit of her wanted a little attention from her new shadow.

Halfway down, she decided that she despised that part of her. It wasn't worth the grazes on her palms or the scuffs on her favorite pair of Gucci sneakers. It certainly wasn't worth the shock, and then the ultimate fall the rest of the way, when a voice echoed over Atlanta's grunts.

"I don't think I've ever seen a fully grown adult shimmy down a drainpipe before. Hats off to you, love."

Atlanta let out a shrill scream as she fell — without any of the grace her mother had been drilling into her since the age of three — to the gravel. The stones dug into her flesh, tearing through her jeans and coating her favorite winter coat with a chalky white. She tried to dust it off before checking her hands for injuries. They were slightly bloodied and still bore the imprint of the plastic trellis she had used as makeshift ladder rungs, but she hadn't fallen as far as she'd initially thought. The cold slicing into her made everything sting a little more than it would have otherwise.

Finally she stood up on unsteady feet and glared at the bodyguard watching her. Beck had her arms crossed, her features as blank as they had been since the moment she'd arrived. Atlanta couldn't say why that unwillingness to show any sort of emotion bothered her so much. "Where did you come from?"

Beck pointed upward, and Atlanta followed the motion to a small security camera hidden beneath her bedroom balcony. "I have eyes and ears everywhere. Going somewhere?"

"No." Atlanta smirked mischievously as she examined Beck. She wasn't as put-together as she had been earlier, with the top button of her shirt undone and her straight hair loose across her shoulders. Had she been hoping for an early night? She could say goodbye to those if she wanted to follow Atlanta around. "I just thought it was a nice night for a climb."

"Listen, there's no need to sneak around like a teenager." Atlanta did not appreciate the hoarse reproach in Beck's words. "You're not a child and I'm not your mother."

"No," Atlanta observed, propping herself up by the wall and crossing her ankles. "My mother has a lot more Botox and isn't nearly as pretty."

Beck's tongue slid across her bottom lip as she slanted her head. "My looks are the least interesting thing about me, Atlas."

Atlas? Was Beck seriously pretending that she didn't even know Atlanta's name? "Atlanta."

"Sorry?"

Atlanta frowned curiously, no longer certain whether Beck was messing with her or not. She kept her composure so perfectly in place that it was difficult to tell — and since Atlanta's new favorite hobby was trying to break that composure, it was quite an inconvenience. "My name is Atlanta."

"Is it?" Beck feigned confusion and then shrugged. "My mistake."

"What happened to 'miss,' anyway?"

"You asked me not to call you that, didn't you?"

Atlanta raised her eyebrows, teeth beginning to chatter as a gust of wind cut through her. Beck didn't so much as flinch, though she wore fewer layers and a much thinner jacket. *Is this woman made of* stone? Atlanta wondered, disappointment dancing in her belly.

Even if she hadn't reacted to any of Atlanta's attempts to rattle her so far, though, she was entertaining to say the least. Perhaps her dry sense of humor was even better than somebody who fussed and worried or lost their temper. In fact, Beck Harris might just be the most interesting person Atlanta had met in a long time. Atlanta couldn't figure her out, couldn't see past the carefully strung veil of professionalism and arrogance, and that only made her want to claw through to what lay beneath it all even more.

"I guess I did," she replied finally.

"So," Beck muttered, "where are we off to?"

"Oh, it's 'we' now, is it?"

"That's what I'm paid for, love," Beck retorted with a crooked, disbelieving smile of her own. Her teeth were perfectly straight, though the front two were a little larger than the rest. At the way they grazed the plump flesh of her bottom lip, heat surged through Atlanta. She was much more attractive than the balding, middle-aged men they usually sent for security. "I'm not stopping you from going about your usual routine. If you want to put yourself in danger for the sake of a party, that's your prerogative. But I will have to follow you... hope I won't cramp your style too much."

Atlanta snorted. "The fact that you would even say 'cramp your style' says plenty. How old are you, forty?"

"I'm old enough."

Atlanta frowned at the evasion of the question, curiosity fluttering within her. She wanted to know more about her — she couldn't help it.

Sighing, she glanced past the wrought-iron fence to the open hills. They were so different from the ones surrounding her California house: those were all rocky and the color of sand. These ones were grassy and rich with dark soil: the picturesque countryside that Atlanta had only ever seen in Jane Austen adaptations before now. They had served as a comfort these past few nights, though they weren't quite home.

The nearest hamlet peppered the night with light a few miles away. Atlanta only knew about the small village because she had been desperate to get out of the house the previous evening and her Google Maps app had alerted her to the nearby bar. It wasn't much, but it was small enough that the scarce handful of patrons hadn't seemed to recognize her.

"There are no parties in the middle of nowhere, anyway," she said finally. "There is, however, a bar down there."

She motioned toward the town, and Beck followed her gaze skeptically. Taking a step back, Beck gestured in offering. "Then by all means, love. After you."

Atlanta grinned and curled her dangling cashmere scarf around her neck so that it wouldn't drag across the floor. "I don't suppose you get paid to drive me, too?"

A scoff fell from Beck as the crunch of her footsteps accompanied Atlanta's own through the gravel. "Funnily enough, Miss Stone, chauffeuring you around does come with the job description. Lucky you."

＊ ＊ ＊

The Messy Pigeon was an apt name for the pub that Atlanta had directed Beck to, considering the courtyard and picnic tables outside were sullied with bird droppings visible beneath the guttering streetlamp. There wasn't much else to see in the hamlet save for a few farms, a corner shop, and a library that had been boarded up. Beck had no idea how an American celebrity could wish to visit a place like this, but Atlanta seemed not to notice any of it as she got out of the car and disappeared into the pub without a second glance back.

Beck turned off the engine, muttering, "Bloody actresses," beneath her breath before she followed the actress inside.

Thankfully, the interior wasn't any worse — but it certainly wasn't all that better. Though the tables were free of animal feces, cigarette smoke snaked around a group of old men sitting in the corner, despite the no-smoking signs, and it was so musty that Beck grappled with a choke when it hit the back of her throat. The few customers were old and weathered, their faces like sun-dried tomatoes that suggested years of having nothing to do but nurse their beer and tan in the summer. At least none of them were likely to know who Atlanta Stone was, and even if they were, they were too invested in their frothing pint glasses to so much as look up when Beck entered after her. Christmas garlands still draped across the windows, though they were well into January now, and an artificial tree bare of its baubles and tinsel cowered sadly in the far corner.

Atlanta had already made herself comfortable on a stool at the far end of the bar, as incongruous as a red rose among dandelions as she ordered from the beak-nosed bartender. Beck caught the end of her request and rolled her eyes: two shots of tequila. As she rounded the bar, wafting the smoke away from her face, the barman placed two pints of beer in front of her, too.

"I didn't peg you as a beer girl," Beck noted as she sat beside her. The stool was hard and cold, and she shifted uncomfortably.

"I thought your job was to hover in the background, not sit with me in plain sight." Atlanta took a sip of the ale as though to prove herself. A foamy white moustache gathered on her top lip, and she wiped it away with her coat sleeve quickly. It was perhaps the strangest sight that Beck had ever witnessed — and that was saying something.

"Oh, I'm sorry, love." Beck smirked. "Were you saving this seat for a friend?"

"You know, I heard so much about British humor before I came here. Then I realized it's just sarcasm, and sarcasm is the lowest form of wit."

"I wouldn't expect you to be able to handle it."

Atlanta scoffed but slid the second pint over

to Beck. Beck pushed it back forcefully, the amber liquid slopping onto the bar.

"Still working."

"Right." Atlanta's brown eyes glittered in the bar's dim lighting, her lashes long enough to kiss the freckles smattering her cheekbones. She was pretty: Beck would give her that. She could see the resemblance to her mother, now, with her button nose and rosebud lips, and she could see why the world might fall in love with her. What teemed beneath the surface of that beauty, though? Anything at all?

It was a question Beck always secretly wished she knew the answer to, with all her clients. Did they rely on their looks and wealth to get by, or did they have talents, passions, stories like she did? If they did, would that make Beck's job feel more worthwhile?

"So." Atlanta loosed a bored breath, running her dainty fingers across the rim of her pint as the two tequila shots were placed in front of her. No lime or salt. "How did you become a bodyguard, Beck Harris?"

Beck braced her elbows against the bar. The outdoor chill had burrowed itself into her jacket, and she had to fight against her shiver. "Why? Looking for a career change?"

"Do you ever give straight answers?"

Sensing her irritation, Beck cast her eyes down as she traced rings across a sticky bar mat with her nail. "I was in the military for a while.

When I came back, I figured I might as well do something I'm good at."

"Like protecting people." Surprise weakened Atlanta's words, and for once, it felt as though Beck had earned her full attention. There was no flirting or joking, no attempt to rattle Beck or make her flustered. It was just the two of them, sitting in a pub, talking. Beck didn't usually do that with her friends in London, let alone a bloody celebrity.

At the realization, her face shuttered. Atlanta was her *client*, and any weakness she showed tonight might very well bite her on the arse later on — especially with somebody like her, who got a kick out of playing with her. "I suppose."

Atlanta downed her first shot without flinching. Beck would have been impressed, but more than anything, it irritated her. No matter what she had said to Atlanta earlier, there was every chance she was still in danger, still a target. The last thing Beck needed was a drunk liability on her hands when all she wanted was to get her job done.

"What's with the name, anyway? Surely your parents didn't just call you Beck."

"Surely your parents didn't just call you Atlanta," Beck retorted, glaring as she caved and took a sip of the beer. Only a sip, though. She still had to get the woman home in one piece, and it wouldn't surprise her if Atlanta made it as difficult as possible.

"My mother is called Minerva." The second

shot went down, and Atlanta slapped the glass on the bar as though victorious. "Work it out."

Beck let out a small laugh. "Well, yeah, there is that."

"Is it short for something? Beck?"

"No." She shook her head. "I chose it myself. It just felt… right, I suppose."

"Your given name didn't?"

"Nope." She popped the *P*, swirling the coaster around with her finger absently. "It was too girly. I think my mum wanted me to be a little bit more… feminine. She forced me into flowery dresses and pigtails until I had a tantrum and told her I wanted a new name."

Atlanta's peal of laughter, musical and loud against the subdued atmosphere, surprised Beck. "That's tragic."

"Imagine how happy she would be that I wear suits and carry a gun for a living."

"Every mother's dream." And then, as though realizing, Atlanta quieted. "She's not around anymore?"

Beck's gaze snapped up at the sound of glass shattering, thoughts of her mother instantly forgotten. Instinctively, her hand fell to her gun in fear that Atlanta had been recognized. All she found, though, was the old barman with shards of glass at his feet.

"Jumpy," Atlanta observed as though Beck's reaction had delighted her.

"It's my job."

"God help you when we get to London tomorrow, if you're this paranoid in a small-town bar."

"I'm sure I'll be just fine," Beck muttered aggravatedly, raising an eyebrow at the barman as he let out a string of curse words before he collected his dustpan and brush. The glass jangled as he swept it up, and then the quiet returned.

"So what is it, then?" Atlanta's cheeks puffed out as she took another swig of beer.

"What's what?"

"Your real name."

Beck snorted. "None of your business."

"Cynthia?" Atlanta guessed. "Annabelle? No, you don't look like either of those.... Oh, god, it's not something floral like Daisy, is it?"

It was difficult for Beck to suppress a laugh. "None of those, but thank you for reminding me how much worse it could have been."

Atlanta pouted. "I'll keep it a secret. Please?"

"No," Beck replied sternly.

Sighing, Atlanta pulled her phone from her coat pocket and began to scroll, her golden face awash in Twitter's pale blue light. Beck swallowed down her bitter grunt and fiddled with an ashtray filled with peanuts instead.

A mangled gasp of disgust caught in Atlanta's throat as her thumb hovered over her screen. "Ugh. Man-whore."

Beck could not summon the energy to feign interest until Atlanta forced the phone under her nose. She scowled but took it, inspecting the picture on the screen. It was an Instagram post depicting a dark-haired, shirtless man with a neatly trimmed beard and an expensive watch on show, gruesomely attached to the face of a blonde-haired girl who might have been Atlanta's double if not for the fact that she still looked like a teenager. The comments beneath the nonsensical caption were littered with fire emojis and capital letters that Beck couldn't piece into coherent sentences.

"Who is he?"

"You don't know him?" Atlanta tore the phone away, her eyes wide in shock as she buried her fingers into the bowl of peanuts. She shoved the whole handful into her mouth with none of the grace an actress was expected to have.

"Oh yeah, come to think of it, this bloke and I are good pals."

Atlanta shot her a withering look as she chewed. "You seriously didn't know who I was before, did you?"

"I know what I need to know: you're my client. Sorry if that bruises your ego."

"It's not about my ego," she bit back. "My face is plastered all over every magazine and social media platform at least twice a month. Usually when I'm drunk or with him." She jabbed her finger into her phone, the sharp scent of the tequila clinging to her breath and wafting over Beck. "Do you live under a rock? Are we not paying you enough to afford Wi-Fi?"

Beck rolled her eyes. For a moment she had forgotten who Atlanta was, and how self-absorbed it made her. She was quite grateful for the little reminder. "I don't follow celebrity culture. I have better things to do."

"Right. You just let us pay your bills."

"I think it was *your* family who asked for *my* help, love," Beck snarled, irritation prickling at her. "Not the other way around."

She had never spoken to a client like this before, but she couldn't help it. Atlanta Stone was getting under her skin, and Beck wasn't about to just sit and take it because she was famous.

"God, you're so touchy tonight," Atlanta breathed, holding her hands up in surrender. "If you were a guy, I would have said you were overcompensating."

"If I were a guy, you wouldn't be trying to mess with me the way you are."

"Oh" — she laughed humorlessly — "believe me, I would. You would have slept with me by now, too."

Beck raised an eyebrow, leaning forward in her chair. "If you were trying to get me into bed, love, all you had to do was say."

"Is that an offer?" It was a joke — at least, Beck hoped it was a bloody joke — but Atlanta's eyes gleamed as though daring her. Beck shook her head and broke their gaze, realizing that the pub had emptied and only the two of them were left save for the man behind the bar, who was still cleaning up his mess while he moaned and groaned.

Beck huffed quietly and pointed at Atlanta's phone still faceup on the bar with the picture of the grinning man. "Who is he, then? An ex?"

"Investigating my sexual history before you agree?" Atlanta taunted, chewing on her lip in a way that Beck knew must have led men to unravel in front of her. Beck held strong, ignoring the soft red of her lips and the way she seemed to glow even in a setting as dreary as this one. "Smart."

"I want to know if I need to keep him away from you," Beck replied stonily.

"Afraid you can't compete?"

Beck stared at her, unblinking.

Atlanta slumped in surrender. "Technically, he's an ex. He was more of a publicity stunt for me, though. Not that that stops him from drunk-calling me most nights like a pathetic little baby. Hugo Dean is his name. He's a musician-slash-model."

"He looks like an arse-slash-hole," Beck noted, getting a final glimpse of him so that she could store him in her memory for later. It wouldn't have been the first time she'd had to protect her client from a jealous ex, and it was a precaution she wouldn't make the mistake of not taking.

"Is that your professional opinion?" Atlanta finished the last dregs of her beer and put the glass down. Beck was impressed she wasn't even tipsy after the shots and the full pint. Then again, if she was used to drinking, her tolerance was probably much higher than some of the other spoiled, sloppy brats Beck had worked for.

"Yes, it is, Miss Stone."

"I prefer it when you call me love, Miss Harris." Atlanta pushed away from the bar and hopped to her feet with the throwaway comment. Beck pretended she didn't hear it. She cursed in disbelief when Atlanta began to make her way out without paying for the drinks, and searched in her pocket for a ten-pound note. She found a crumpled one in the back of her jeans and threw it down on the bar before marching out after the blonde.

"Don't get used to me paying for your shit, *love*." Beck put emphasis on the word, and it dripped with the resentment that had been bubbling in her all day.

"Didn't I pay?" Atlanta flashed Beck an innocent look as she leaned against her car patiently. "My bad."

"Considering you probably earn ten times my annual salary in an hour, it is your bad." Beck opened the door. Protocol usually had her opening the passenger door for her client first, but since the street was dead and she was pissed off, she didn't bother. Instead she slid into the driver's seat and thrust her keys into the ignition without waiting for Atlanta. The actress hopped in a moment later, looking amused. Her nose was smattered pink from the cold.

"Don't feel inadequate, *love*," Atlanta

mocked in a way that made Beck want to let out a string of foully worded insults that would surely get her fired. "We can't all get paid for being talented and beautiful."

"Oh, believe me," Beck growled, clenching the steering wheel until her knuckles turned white, "sitting next to you, I've never felt more adequate."

"Is that right?" The flirtatiousness returned to Atlanta's voice as she raked her hand through her wavy hair, letting it fall strategically across the side of her face as though she were a model posing for a lingerie photoshoot.

Beck sucked in a deep breath to quell her anger before the engine rumbled to life. If it did come to it, she was beginning to think that it would be more difficult to protect Atlanta than let her face the danger. In fact, the thought of having to save somebody so entitled, so irritating, was almost unthinkable at present.

"That's right, Miss Stone." Beck's words were frosty, detached, but still steady as she pulled out of the carpark. Atlanta Stone would not get under her skin — no matter how hell-bent she was on trying.

FOUR

The Langham Hotel was situated in Marylebone — a part of London that Beck ventured into only when she was forced to pass through it, mostly because it was full of posh people who looked down their noses at her. Today it swarmed with fancy-suited businesspeople armed with briefcases and choked by tightly knotted ties. Beck had time to kill before she met up with Atlanta later, since Eric and Phil were escorting the family from their country home back into the city, and when instinct had led her here, she had decided not to question it.

She examined the large building, trying to picture it in the early hours of the morning. It was an enormous, castle-like place, forged with marble walls inside, old architecture out. Security cameras swiveled their robotic eyes across every corner of the lobby. Pots and pans clattered behind Beck from the low-lit restaurant, the rich, earthy aroma of coffee beans waking her up enough to focus more intently — especially on the back wall, where the faint outline of a door blended in with the stone.

Beck scanned her vicinity a final time to be

sure she was not being watched before weaving through the hotel guests and pushing it open. It was unlocked.

She had expected an office or a corridor. Instead she was brought out to an echoing staircase that led both upstairs and down. A fire exit glowed on the opposite side, probably leading out onto the side street she had glimpsed on the way in. If an armed robber was to attempt an attack in a hotel like this one, she would wager that this would be the least conspicuous way of entering — especially if they knew to come in through the fire exit from the alleyway.

And yet it wasn't that inconspicuous at all, she saw a moment later, because there were just as many cameras in here as there were in the lobby, hidden behind floral arrangements and dark corners. Nobody would have come in this way without being spotted.

Unless they had known that the security footage would have been conveniently lost that night. Unless, somehow, they had planned for it. Unless it was an inside job.

Beck fell back out into the lobby with questions and possibilities still dancing in her mind. There was no longer a queue at the front desk, and Beck took that as an opportunity. A middle-aged gray-haired man stood behind the computer, glasses perched on his nose as he typed something onto his keyboard. Beck cleared her throat and leaned presumptuously against the counter.

The man looked up. She scanned his shirt for a name tag and found one pinned to his breast pocket. Frederik. He didn't look like a Frederik, really, his features darker and longer than any Frederik's or Fred's that Beck had ever come across.

"Can I help you, madam?" Frederik questioned in a very southern, very false, stuffy British accent.

"Yes, actually. I have some questions about an incident that occurred here recently. My clients were targeted in an armed robbery, and they were attacked in their rooms."

Frederik paled, though he kept his best customer-service grin pasted across his face. Beck would bet that he thought her the inevitable lawyer come to sue the place — if one hadn't already — and found a slight hint of amusement in the fact. "Regretfully, the manager isn't in the building this morning, but I'm certain he would be happy to —"

"Were you working the night of the robbery, sir?" Beck interrupted, cutting him off with a quick raise of her hand.

"No, madam, I was not." The stray whiskers on his chin wobbled.

"Is there anybody here that was? A security guard or a housekeeper, perhaps?"

Frederik's face shuttered with a steely guardedness, and for a moment Beck thought she wouldn't get another word out of him. Then he gestured across the lobby. "I believe George, our porter over there, was working the early-morning shift that night."

Beck followed his line of sight and saw another tall man in a suit helping a guest with their bags.

"Great." She flashed a smile and patted the counter appreciatively. "Thank you, Fred."

Frederik's glare pricked into her spine as she turned and approached the porter, waiting patiently for him to finish a conversation about seagulls in the middle of London with a heavily accented Italian tourist. Finally the tourist took her bags and bid George a throaty "*Ciao.*"

George turned and came face-to-face with Beck. He was older than Frederik, his face dotted with age spots and creased by deep-set wrinkles. Like Frederik's, his eyes were guarded — more so when he almost crashed into her.

"Hello, George. Have you got a minute?"

"How may I help you, madam?" His words were taut, as though he already sensed that Beck was not a guest, but something else entirely. They'd probably had weeks of visits from the police, and perhaps even MI5 if the situation warranted it.

"I was told you were working on the morning of the armed robbery. Is that correct?"

George did not falter. "May I ask who wishes to know?"

"I do, George," Beck stated, deadpan. "My clients were the targets of the attack, and I have a few questions."

"I've told the police everything I can." George fidgeted with his spotless white gloves, a flush of red beginning to creep from the buttoned collar of his shirt and up his sagging neck.

"I'm not working with the police. I'm a close protection officer, and I'd like to understand what happened that night. I was told that the security footage went missing."

"It was lost to an accidental system failure."

Beck raised an eyebrow, taking a step forward. George immediately took one back to maintain the distance between them. "All of it?"

"Unfortunately so, madam."

So very convenient. "Where were you when it happened?"

Under Beck's unwavering stare, George's eyes flitted around helplessly. Satisfaction swelled in her at the fact that she could intimidate a man twice her age, but it also told her what she needed to know: the hotel staff had failed their job somewhere, and perhaps knew something they weren't so keen on revealing.

"I was watching the front desk, madam."

"So you saw nothing? Heard nothing?"

George shook his head, wringing his gloved fingers. "Not a peep until the gunshots."

Beck frowned. "Not even before that?"

"No, madam."

"That's odd, George." Beck cocked her head, thrusting her hands in her pockets. George flinched at that movement alone. "According to the reports, Atlanta Stone came in through the lobby not ten minutes before the attack — quite loudly I'd imagine, too, since she'd been partying with friends."

Sweat began to glisten at the edge of George's receding hairline as he stammered in response. "That's right. I did see Miss Stone a few minutes before. I'd forgotten."

"I'm glad I could jog your memory." Beck smirked dryly. "I hope your story was a little bit more organized for the police, George."

George loosed a nervy breath, glancing out of the corner of his eye again as though pleading for assistance. "I'm sorry, madam. I'm not getting any younger. My brain doesn't recall things quite as well as it used to."

"Look, I can't arrest you or touch you in any way. I work in security, not the force. However, I do want to know how two armed robbers managed to sneak their way into one of the fanciest and most secure hotels in London without anybody noticing... so either you're lying to me about where you were that night for the sake of your job, or you let those men upstairs to steal from my clients. Which is it?"

George's jowls shook as he swallowed, his shoulders slumping in resignation. "All right. Between you and me, madam..."

"Of course, George." Beck's smile dripped with honey, sickly sweet and as convincing as she could make it. She didn't often use being a somewhat attractive woman to her advantage, but it was quite useful every so often.

"I was asleep at the desk," he finally confessed, tongue sliding across stained teeth. "It's very rare we have guests coming and going at four o'clock in the morning, and we have security keeping watch on the CCTV... I'm practically redundant at that time. I didn't think anything bad could come from me having a quick snooze."

From the way that his voice strained desperately, Beck could tell that he was telling the truth. She always knew, just as she always spotted a lie. She sighed with chagrin, her posture softening to signal that the interrogation was over. George sagged with relief.

"How many security guards do you have on duty during the night?"

"Just the two in the office, and others on standby in the main office if need be. They claimed to see nothing suspicious on the monitors until it was too late."

Beck shook her head, clenching her jaw in irritation. It didn't make sense. None of it made sense. "Maybe they fancied a snooze, too." She opened her mouth with the intention to thank George, but froze at the sound of her name being called behind her.

"Harris?"

She whirled quickly on her heel to find Michael Carson, another one of her colleagues, dressed in far more casual attire than his usual uniform. "Michael," she greeted with a confused nod. "What brings you here?"

"I, er" — Carson checked his watch impatiently — "I have a meeting with a client. What are you doing here? I thought you'd been assigned to a new family."

"I have," Beck replied. "The Stones."

Carson ran a large hand across the short bristles of his dark hair. "The family who were caught up in that shooting?"

"An armed robbery," she elaborated. "And it happened here."

"Did it?" He scratched at the stubble peppering his chin, looking around the place in surprise. "Wow. I had no idea."

Beck shrugged, shifting when her phone began to vibrate in the pocket of her jeans. She had opted for casual attire today so as not to draw attention to herself or Atlanta, clad in a leather jacket and her most stretchy black jeans for the flight to LA tonight. "I have to go, actually, but I'll catch you up on it all when I'm back in the office."

"Yeah, do," he responded, inclining his head in goodbye. "Maybe we can get a drink when you're back. Happy babysitting the celebs."

Beck rolled her eyes as she slid her phone out of her pocket and saw that Atlanta was calling. "Definitely. I have to go. See you later." As she turned, she found George still standing uncomfortably behind her, and she patted him on the shoulder. "Thanks, George. You've been a big help."

It wasn't entirely — or at all — true, but it was the only politeness Beck could muster as she sauntered out of the hotel and onto the gray streets of London.

* * *

Atlanta had no real idea where she was going, but St. Pancras train station seemed as good a way to make her new personal bodyguard squirm as any. Beck had been following her around since brunch, and Atlanta had time to kill while her brother met up with an old friend and her mother and Weston threw their money at another set of pearls or diamonds. She was bored of dreary, rainy London.

Paris Gare du Nord, on the other hand, she thought as she eyed the Eurostar departures board, sounded quite interesting.

She flashed a look to Beck over her shoulder. The woman hovered a few meters away so as not to draw any attention to Atlanta, and it had worked so far. Apparently she wasn't that famous in London yet — or maybe British people didn't expect American celebrities to walk their streets. Either way, Atlanta wasn't complaining. She had enjoyed the peacefulness of disappearing into the crowd.

Even if that peace was often shattered by the backing track of Beck's boots thumping in time with her own steps against the concrete as she walked.

"How's your French, Miss Harris?" Atlanta asked finally.

"*Probablement mieux que le vôtre.*" The response surprised Atlanta — pleasantly. Her pronunciation of the words was guttural and low, dripping like caramel from soft, curled lips. And Atlanta knew from years of being homeschooled by a French tyrant what they meant: *Probably better than yours.*

She raised an eyebrow, smirking. "Touché."

Beck only blinked blankly. "I told you last night that I'm not your babysitter, Miss Stone, but I do feel compelled to remind you that you have a red-eye back to LA tonight."

Atlanta shrugged, tucking her handbag beneath her arm as she contemplated. "I believe my work schedule is clear until next week, and I'm sure there are just as many flights to LAX from Charles de Gaulle as there are from Heathrow."

"And I suppose if I advised you to keep a low profile, I'd be wasting my breath."

Anticipation shot through Atlanta all at once. She could do this, and nobody could stop her. She had been to Paris only once before, for fashion week, but had had barely any time to take in the city properly. A freedom she had never felt before yawned out in front of her, humming in time with train engines and conversation.

But she had to be quick. The Eurostar was due to leave in just over half an hour.

"I assume you have your passport?"

Beck searched her jacket pocket and waved around the proof with a wary expression.

"Good. Then I think we'll go to Paris, Miss Harris...." Atlanta paused, grinning. "Hey, that rhymes."

"Indeed," Beck replied dryly. "Sounds like a lovely little children's book, Miss Stone. Perhaps you should note it down in case you ever fancy a change in career."

It might have been more of that British "humor," but Atlanta didn't think it sounded like a bad idea at all.

FIVE

Beck soon found out that Atlanta's new endeavor into tourism consisted mainly of shopping. From the Gare du Nord, she had ordered an Uber to take them straight to "the nearest Chanel store." Beck was glad that she had already been to Paris more than a few times, and so wasn't too disappointed when she realized that the more scenic spots were not on today's agenda. Still, after stumbling out of the third shop on Avenue Montaigne behind Atlanta, a Gucci bag in one hand and a Dior in the other, she was more than a little bored of the entire thing.

And Atlanta knew it. While trying on new shoes or testing a sample of perfume, Atlanta often cast amused glances in Beck's direction as though she were doing this only to piss her off. It was beginning to work — especially since she dragged the entire thing out, spending ten minutes examining one dress before putting it down, moving onto another, and repeating the whole ordeal.

Beck wondered if it had even occurred to the woman that the money she had spent on one handbag was enough to feed the entire population of homeless people in the city or house multiple families in poverty. She wondered if she thought of them at all. She wondered, more than anything, how Atlanta slept at night on a bed of wealth while some people couldn't afford the basic necessities.

The more that Beck caught whiffs of sickly sweet perfumes and passed through air-conditioning vents whose cold breaths made her dizzy, the more she began to feel nauseous with it, her upper lip gradually curling upward in distaste until it stuck there.

Still, it wasn't her job to judge, so she followed Atlanta down the avenue and into the next shop: a huge Saint Laurent, white-paneled and lined with wrought-iron fencing. It was twice as large as Beck's apartment in London, and probably held a million times more value.

The inside confirmed it. The smell of soft leather hit her with enough force to make her want to walk straight back out. Instead she followed behind Atlanta sourly as the actress greeted the assistants with her nose in the air, making sure that they knew she was important and should be treated as such.

It was difficult to believe that only last night, Atlanta had been sitting in a musty old bar among people who had probably worked all their life and still had no designer handbags or fancy boots to show for it. She fit right in here, with her sharp *Bonjour*s and her new Prada sunglasses perched on her head.

In her tattered denim jeans and a leather jacket snatched from a Primark sale last year, Beck could not say the same of herself. A sigh, rough with aggravation, weighed on her chest, and she risked letting it out when Atlanta picked up a third blazer — identical, Beck thought, to the other two she had just put down.

"Is there a problem, Miss Harris?" Atlanta seemed pleased she could finally ask as she returned the blazer to the racks with a sharp clattering of metal against metal.

Beck took up her position by the mirror, crossing her hands and swaying on her heels lightly. "No problem, Miss Stone."

Atlanta motioned with her free hand to the collection of plain professional attire before her. "I thought you liked black. You wear it often enough."

"Fashion advice isn't in my job description, as far as I recall," Beck retorted, speaking in a low voice so the shop assistants wouldn't hear them bicker.

"I'm not asking for myself." Atlanta shrugged and pulled out another — identical — blazer. "You'd be about a UK size twelve, right?"

Beck's eyebrows knitted together in confusion. "Excuse me?"

Atlanta peeled the blazer from the coat hanger and held it out to Beck with a smirk. "Try it on. See how it fits."

"I'm not your new Barbie doll, love." Beck

scowled down at the blazer as though it were something rotten. "I'm not playing dress-up with you."

"But you're in dire need of some new clothes." Atlanta's eyes flitted down Beck's figure as though proving her point.

Beck gritted her teeth, anger beginning to simmer beneath her façade. Usually she was able to stay calm in any situation, but Atlanta Stone really was beginning to test her patience. She had survived war before now and not felt so rattled. "My clothes are fine."

"Bless you for believing that," Atlanta taunted with vicious sympathy. "Please, I insist. Try it on."

Beck shook her head with a huff. Atlanta's eyes glittered wickedly. She wouldn't give up. Beck could have remained stubborn, could have stood in the shop for the rest of the day, staring the impossible woman down until she shrank away — but she wanted to get out of this shop, and it was becoming clear that Atlanta could be just as persistent as she was.

One of them had to cave first, and Beck wanted to leave this place enough for it to be her. So she put her pride aside and shrugged off her jacket, seizing the blazer from Atlanta's hands with more than a little aggression. Atlanta's dark eyes explored the black turtleneck that clung to Beck's figure unabashedly. It had felt modest when she had tucked it into her belt this morning. Now, beneath Atlanta's gaze, she wondered if the material stretched too thinly over her curves. Her revolver was kept in the holster at her hip, and she was careful not to turn around and flash it to the shop assistants as she slid the blazer on.

It did fit well — she would give Atlanta that. It was slightly oversized in the arms, the sleeves rolled at the wrist and the style double-breasted. Beck turned to the mirror behind her, freeing the ends of her hair from the collar and crossing her arms impatiently. She pretended not to notice that for all her silent complaining, the blazer looked quite good on her. She felt more herself in it, with the padded shoulders broadening her frame and the tail skimming the back of her thighs. If she weren't on duty, and if it were about one thousand six hundred and fifty euros cheaper, she might have actually considered buying it. "Happy?"

Atlanta admired her with a sly smile. "Very."

Beck rolled her eyes and took it off, passing it back to her with a grunt. She expected Atlanta to put the blazer back on the rack, but instead she carried it to the till, where a shop assistant waited. "I hope you're not buying that for me."

"Think of it as your employer providing your work uniform," Atlanta said dismissively, pulling her credit card out of her purse. Beck could only imagine how much money she had on that thing — how many zeroes.

"You're not my employer. Your mother is."

"Well, my mom is the source of most of my

money anyway, so there we go." Atlanta punched her pin number into the card reader and the receipt was spat out. She smiled falsely at the assistant as she handed the bag to Beck before turning on her heel and walking straight out of the store.

Beck scoffed in disbelief and followed her out, seething with frustration.

Atlanta was already scouring the tree-lined avenue for her next victim. "All right, where to next?"

"Atlanta." It might have been the first time Beck had used her first name, but she was no longer thinking about professionalism. It was an effort just to keep her voice steady.

"What?" Atlanta asked innocently.

"You might as well return that now." Beck pointed down at the bag. "I'm not wearing a one-thousand-euro blazer."

"I know you're not." She arched an eyebrow smugly. "You're wearing a one-thousand-seven-hundred-euro blazer. Do you want to wear it now?"

"What game are you trying to play with me?" Back glanced around, ensuring that there was nobody else to witness the interaction before she leaned in close to Atlanta — close enough that she could smell the minty chewing gum on her breath.

Atlanta remained unfazed — a fact that only infuriated Beck more. "I'm not playing a game, Miss Harris."

"Then take the bloody blazer back. Now. I'm

not your charity case."

Atlanta's eyes narrowed. "Is that what you think this is? Have I hurt your precious pride?"

"My pride is just fine, love," Beck snarled. "Look, I'll do my job. I'll humor you. I'll follow you around for hours while you do everything but keep a low profile because you care more about your outfit than the fact that you might actually be in danger. But don't think for a minute that you can play me as your puppet, Stone. I'm not a part of your world. I don't want your fancy clothes and I certainly don't want to be your new distraction from the eternal tedium that comes with being a vapid, rich little celebrity who'll wind up a washed-up nobody in a few years' time. I'm not your new toy. You'd better stop treating me like I am."

Atlanta bit down on her smirk, forehead wrinkling as she took a step back. Beck couldn't tell if she was upset or impressed — she was too busy instantly regretting her outburst. It had been anything but professional.

And yet it had been what Atlanta wanted — she could tell that from the satisfaction smoothing her features now. She loved nothing more than to get under Beck's skin, and it had worked. Beck had given her the upper hand, like an idiot.

"I just thought the blazer looked good on you," Atlanta said finally with a shrug. "I'm sorry it upset you so much. If you don't want it, fine. I'll keep it for myself."

"I don't."

"Fine." Atlanta shook her head, blonde hair curling up against the brisk wind. "You really can't stand me, can you?"

"It's not my job to like you." Beck finally took a step back, paper bags rustling in her hands. "It's my job to protect you."

Atlanta tilted her head to the side. "And how can I expect you to do that if you hate me? What would be your motive for saving my life, other than the fact that my mother will pay you for it?"

"I suppose you'll just have to trust me, Miss Stone." Beck flashed a toothy, withering grin and slid on her sunglasses. "Are we done here?"

"Yes," Atlanta sighed, and set off back down the avenue without warning. "We're done here."

❊ ❊ ❊

Atlanta could feel Beck hovering behind her like a fly as she tore into the large, lace-trimmed box of macarons, her legs dangling over the edge of the walkway. It wasn't exactly a nutritional dinner, but she didn't feel like eating in a restaurant alone for fear of being recognized, and she was certain she could get something from the airport later on.

For now, she wanted to drink up her last few hours in Paris while the sun sank into the River Seine.

She placed the macarons beside her along

with the two hot chocolates she'd bought from one of the backstreet cafes and turned to look at Beck over her shoulder. Beck pretended she hadn't noticed the attention, standing in her usual rigid posture as she glared out at the water. It felt infinite down here, wending beneath the arches of the Pont Neuf bridge in a ribbon of deep blue mottled with gray. Atlanta wished she could stay.

"You're allowed to sit beside me, you know." Atlanta warmed her frostbitten fingers with her cup. "Help me eat these macarons."

Beck pursed her lips, her eyes a piercing gold that mirrored the color of the bleeding sky. "No, thank you."

"Oh, come on." Atlanta rolled her eyes and nudged the box further toward her. "I bought them for both of us… or are you too good for my dessert as well as my clothes?"

Glaring, Beck sat down, crossing her legs and accepting the hot drink that Atlanta held out for her without thanks. Not that Atlanta had been expecting any. She picked out a vanilla macaron and bit into it, licking her lips when sugary flakes dusted them. They were good, she supposed, but now she wished she had bought croissants instead.

"What's your flavor of choice, Beck Harris?"

"Wouldn't you like to know?" Beck tucked her hair behind her ear and watched a crowd across the river warily. Atlanta didn't know why. Not one person had recognized her all day, even in the bustling heart of Paris. She doubted they would catch on now with a wide body of water separating them.

"It's why I asked." Atlanta narrowed her eyes as she scanned the pastel-colored treats, and then the list of flavors on the card they came with. They were all in French, but she could decipher enough. "I'd guess something horrifyingly boring, like coffee or mint."

"You'd guess wrong." The corner of Beck's mouth twitched with the beginnings of a smirk. "In fact, I've never had a macaron, but I can guarantee the last flavors I'd choose would be those ones."

Atlanta gasped in disbelief, putting her hand to her chest dramatically. "No. You've never had one? Ever?"

"Nope. Never."

"Well, we're in Paris. Where better to try your first one?" She shoved the box into Beck's lap. "Might I recommend the salted caramel." She pointed to the pale-brown one with a soft, gooey center. "Go on, then."

Beck picked it up, eyeing it with trepidation before nibbling at the edge. Her brows rose in pleasant surprise. "Not bad, actually."

Atlanta nodded proudly and grabbed a chocolate one. "See. You can cross it off your bucket list now."

"Oh, thank god," Beck replied. Atlanta tried not to notice the way her tongue swiped along her plump bottom lip when she was finished, or the way she licked cream from her thumb. "I was worried that was one dream I'd never fulfill."

Atlanta rolled her eyes at the sarcasm, glancing up as seagulls began to hover and squawk with their wings beating against the wind. *Don't you dare poop on me*, she warned them silently, shooting them a threatening glare. She had only gotten her hair cut and recolored a few days ago. "You know, I only spent my day shopping to annoy the hell out of you."

"Oh, I know," Beck said, taking another sip of the hot chocolate. "You're not that subtle, love."

Love. Every time Beck called her that, something sparked low in Atlanta's stomach, even if it was usually said with condescension. "Aren't I?"

Beck gave her a sideways glance that told her enough. "You're determined to make my job as unpleasant as possible, aren't you?"

"You think I'm a typical spoiled little dumb-blonde actress." Atlanta shrugged.

"So to prove me wrong, you had me traipse around Prada carrying your bags."

"I don't need to prove you wrong." Atlanta pulled her faux-fur coat tighter around herself as the sun's rays fragmented behind the bridge, leaving them cast in shade. "I don't have to prove anything to you. If that's what you choose to see in me, that's what I'll show you."

She could see the tic of a muscle in Beck's square jaw as she swallowed. "Fair enough, I suppose."

It was getting easier to talk to her. Atlanta noticed it, noticed Beck's stony resolve crumbling, her posture softening. She didn't know why it mattered: she didn't care what anybody else thought of her. She slept soundly at night knowing her underwear was plastered on the front of the tabloids and people were talking about her latest hookup all over Twitter.

But she didn't want Beck to be one of those people. She didn't want Beck to see her for what she pretended to be. For the first time, Atlanta wanted to be more than the mess she had become.

She wouldn't admit that, though. In fact, she needed to shake herself if she was going to start giving a damn now. She *was* a mess. She was happy being a mess. She was happy messing with Beck, too.

Atlanta caught the change in Beck as soon as it came. Beck stiffened, a puppet pulled taut on its string. Her irises glazed into blazing amber stones as something on the bridge caught her attention. Atlanta followed her gaze, her stomach twisting in dread.

And she saw it. A pool of paparazzi had gathered, and they were pointing their cameras straight at Atlanta. They had found her.

Her first instinct was to scoff. Beck's was to stand. "Time to go, Miss Stone?"

Atlanta wouldn't be rushed. She placed her box of macarons in one of her large bags and slid her sunglasses on as a makeshift shield. Beck was already gathering the rest of her bags for her, keeping a careful eye on her surroundings as she did. She froze again a moment later.

"Can we get a move on, please, Miss Stone? You've got a bit of an audience up there."

Cursing, Atlanta glanced up the steps. Another crowd was forming, some with cameras and others clearly fans who wanted to talk to her and screamed for her attention. She took the bags from Beck's hands and straightened her back as nonchalantly as she could before skipping up the stone steps onto the road.

It was mayhem. The further she walked, the more suffocated she was by other bodies. A hand remained on the small of her back, Beck's presence a lingering shadow on her side that kept her headed in the right direction — even if she didn't yet know where that was.

Camera flashes and shutters rent the small space, mingling with screams and pleas, Atlanta's name becoming a chant that never faltered. She could barely breathe. She had done this a million times before... but not since the robbery. Not since she was attacked, shoved, forced face-to-face with the barrel of a gun. Beck's words echoed in her mind: *You saw his face. You're the only one who knows what one of them looks like, who can identify him. That might very well make you his next target, love.*

Every face, then, became his. The paparazzo

under her nose grew stubble, the teenage girl's face twisted into his cruel smirk, the eyes of the man in front of her turned to granite. She had never been afraid before him. She was afraid now. It made her regret the hot chocolate and macarons churning in her stomach.

The only thing anchoring Atlanta to the world outside of it all was Beck's voice. "Step away, please. Clear the way, please." And then, more forcefully: "Excuse me. Move. Thank you."

It became a blur of limbs and voices, until Atlanta was pulled onto a cobbled side street full of crooked little buildings. A bell jingled as Beck pushed her through a door, a woody, musky scent blanketing her in sudden warmth.

A bookstore.

Beck bolted the door and turned the open sign to closed. Slatted shadows slithered across the bookcases as she pulled down the blinds.

Atlanta turned numbly and found an old man staring at her. *"J'étais sur le point de fermer,"* he stuttered out in bewilderment, pulling round-framed glasses from his face and standing from an old wooden stool. A newspaper was crumpled in his hands.

"Pardon, monsieur," Beck replied, inserting herself between Atlanta and the man she assumed was the shop owner. In her daze, Atlanta had no idea what either of them were saying. Her head was floating and flashing, still somewhere else where nothing could touch her. *"Parlez vous an-*

glais?"

The man nodded, graying hair falling across his eyes. "I do."

"Great." Beck sighed in relief. "Does your shop have a back entrance?"

"It does." He frowned, inspecting the two of them with his hands on his hips. "You are looking for any book in particular?"

Atlanta huffed, her pulse still pounding in her ears as she browsed the shelves quickly and picked up a battered copy of *Pride and Prejudice*. She already had a personalized clothbound copy at home, but she knew these sorts of men. He wouldn't help if they didn't make it worth his while. For good measure, she threw in an anthology of Brontë poems and a French cookbook before handing them to him. "These ones."

The man eased immediately as he led her to an old cash register and rang her up. If he recognized her, he didn't show it — though she noticed a magazine rack behind him with her face, airbrushed and dewy, on an old issue of *Vogue*. Atlanta glanced over her shoulder, searching, always, for Beck. Her bodyguard was murmuring softly into her phone by a rack of travel guides: ordering a car, probably.

"Would you mind if we stayed in here for ten minutes or so? I'm waiting for a car to pick me up, and it's mayhem out there."

The man sighed warily, as though Atlanta were asking him to sacrifice a limb, but when she gave him the money, including a very excessive tip, he nodded. "Very well. You are famous?"

She hated that word: *famous*. Not that she'd ever admit it. With a coy smile, she pointed to the *Vogue* magazine. "That's me."

"Oh, you are an actress." He looked only mildly impressed as he glimpsed the cover. "Okay. You can stay. But only ten minutes, *oui*?"

"*Oui*. Thank you, sir. I appreciate it."

"The back entrance is through there." He pointed through the corridor, to where a shaft of light chased away the shadows from an envelope-sized window of a yellow door. "I will be in my office."

"Thank you," Atlanta repeated, juggling the books he passed back to her before remembering her bags. She threw them in carelessly, glad when Beck finally hung up. Her expression was grave as she slid her phone into her pocket.

"A car is on its way. They'll meet us by the back entrance."

"Okay." Atlanta swallowed down the bile that had risen and ran a finger across the worn leather spines on the back shelf. It trembled. Dust floated down with the movement, visible only in the soft rays of light slipping through.

"Are you okay?"

"Fine." Years of acting had made Atlanta good at lying. Still, anxiety writhed in her as though she was still under threat, and the old wound at the back of her head throbbed, though it had been sewn shut weeks ago so that now only a scar remained, hidden by her hair.

"You're used to it, I suppose."

"It happens." She shrugged. "At least now I have big strong Beck to protect me, right?"

She hadn't meant it to come out sarcastically. In fact, it was true. Beck had guided her every step of the way, through men twice the size of them and crowds dense enough to smother them. Even so, misplaced bitterness infected her words, and the frustration radiating from Beck in response prickled against Atlanta's skin.

"Maybe if you were clever enough to keep a low profile like I said, I wouldn't have to."

Atlanta whipped around, cheeks blazing with heat. "So it's my fault that I get followed and attacked and exploited? It's my fault that everyone thinks they have a right to pry into my life?"

"No," Beck said steadily, nostrils flaring, "it's not your fault, but you should be smart enough to know better."

"But I'm not smart, Beck," Atlanta snapped, Beck's name a venomous strike. "I'm vapid, remember?"

A mangled scoff caught in Beck's throat. She shook her head, hands curled into fists. "You're childish, is what you are. You provoked me into saying that and you know it."

"Oh, so you acting unprofessionally with your client is my fault, too." This argument was just a way of distracting Atlanta from the things she didn't want to face: the fear. But she let it continue, let the guttering flames between them continue to blaze. The alternative only hurt more. "I could have you fired."

"Good. Have me fired. I can think of far better ways to be spending my time."

"Like job-hunting?"

"It beats this." Beck murmured the quip under her breath before heading into the hallway. "I'll keep a lookout for the car. You brush your hair or touch up your makeup or whatever it is you do."

Atlanta was practically convulsing in anger. Still, she found the strength to play off Beck's criticism. "Great. Do you have a mirror?"

"Maybe you can use those ridiculously shiny shoes you just wasted ten thousand euros on." Beck's voice floated down the hallway, an overwhelming presence even when out of sight. Atlanta was glad she could no longer see her face. It might soon have been flattened by the huge hardback edition of Shakespeare's plays that Atlanta was currently feigning interest in.

She prayed to god that the car they were waiting for was big enough that she didn't have to look at Beck again today.

❊ ❊ ❊

Night crawled across the city, the black car slinking into its shadows as it weaved away from the lights of Paris, toward the airport. Atlanta hadn't said a word since getting in. Instead she stared out of the tinted windows with her back turned to Beck while the elegant architecture faded into identical gray apartment blocks and hostels. Beck savored the peace, wilting into the leather headrest and letting her eyes fall shut. It was the first moment she'd had to herself all day.

It was exhausting, this life. Even after the military, it weighed on her sometimes just how much time she spent taking care of other people instead of herself. Her head was always droning and busy, body always poised and alert, an engine that was never turned off. She often wondered what would be left when she eventually retired or moved on — who would she be when the keys were pulled from the ignition? If she didn't break down altogether first.

Maybe after this job it would be time for a change. Maybe this would be the last time.

She might have believed it if it weren't a promise she had made and broken a thousand times before.

One day.

"Can you stop the car for a second?"

Beck snapped back to life just as soon as she had drifted from it, her seatbelt pulling against her chest as she straightened. Atlanta pursed her lips as she waited for the answer — no doubt knowing already that the driver wouldn't dare defy her. She was right. He slowed to a stop at the side of the road a moment later. Beck's gaze narrowed, and she curled her hand around Atlanta's wrist as she reached to unclip her seatbelt.

"What are you doing?"

"Simmer down, Harris." Atlanta rolled her eyes and snatched her arm away, unfastening her seatbelt and opening the car door. The cold night air poured in, merciless enough to steal Beck's breath. "I'm just getting one last picture of Paris."

Atlanta looped one of her new scarves around her neck before getting out. Beck huffed before following, coming to a halt in the middle of the road when she found the object of Atlanta's attention.

From here, there was a perfect — albeit distant — view of the Eiffel Tower, lit up and wrapped in twilight. Golden dots twinkled as though wishing them a goodbye, haloing the city in its magic. Beck only realized that she was still in harm's way when a car turned onto the street, and she hopped onto the path quickly, studying Atlanta.

Atlanta didn't look at her. Didn't say a word. The lights danced in her eyes, watery from the cold, and she only stared, swallowed, shivered. There was a sadness there, niggling at the dimple at the corner of her mouth and softening her features until Beck could find nothing of the actress she'd thought she'd known.

For the first time, in the quiet and the dark, Beck saw who Atlanta might really be behind all of her games and jokes. And who she might be was… lonely. Vulnerable.

Beck cleared her throat and looked away, reminding herself that this was a woman who had splashed thousands of euros on designer clothes today just to make her job harder. She didn't need nor deserve Beck's sympathy.

Finally Atlanta sighed and pulled out her phone. "Would you take a picture of me?"

Beck snatched it from her with a roll of her eyes. "I'll add photographer to my growing list of duties, shall I?"

Still, she stepped back to make sure she got both Atlanta and the Eiffel Tower in the frame and snapped a few photos with little interest. Atlanta posed, one leg in front of the other and her lips puckered as she played with her hair.

"There. You can put it on Instagram now, love. Hashtag *narcissist in Paris*."

Atlanta glowered and seized the phone back. "Jealousy doesn't suit you, Miss Harris."

Beck could only snort at the idea of ever being jealous of Atlanta. "You might have money and looks, love, but they won't last forever."

"And what do you have?" Atlanta quipped, raising an eyebrow. "What do you go home to when you're done here, Beck?"

Beck's heart stuttered, but she didn't let it show. Instead she straightened out her jacket and nodded to the black car idling by the curb coldly. "Your flight's in an hour. Might I suggest hurrying up?"

For once, Atlanta didn't need to be told

twice. She got into the car and slammed the door with so much force Beck half expected the windows to splinter from their frames. She shook her head, suppressing a curse, before sliding back in on the opposite side.

Even though Beck kept her features carved into the harsh, neutral expression she had perfected long ago, Atlanta's question burned deep in her gut.

Because it was true.

When this was over, Beck would go home to an empty apartment — just like she always did.

SIX

Being back in LA, with the stifling heat and the even more stifling Minerva Stone, was not something that Atlanta was particularly happy about — even if she was glad to be free of London and all that had happened there.

She still had dreams about it, though. She still had dreams about *him*. She had woken this morning in a cold sweat, her heart thrumming against her ribs until she was certain they would explode.

She needed a distraction.

Unfortunately, her mother had other plans. When Atlanta dragged herself out of her king-size bed at midday after sleeping off her jet lag from the flight the day before — a flight that had been spent mostly in silence, with Beck sitting in the seat behind her, dozing or reading or doing anything that allowed her to ignore Atlanta completely — she was attacked instantly with questions.

"How was Paris?" Minerva's tone was accusatory as she put her magazine down on the kitchen counter.

Atlanta yawned and rolled her eyes, glad to find that there was an acai bowl waiting for her on the breakfast bar. She sat down on her stool and dug in immediately, forgetting her mother's presence until the cool prickle of being observed caused her to pause. Her mother was still waiting, tapping her pointed nails against the counter.

"Paris was fine."

"You could have told me you were going."

Atlanta shrugged, licking the yogurt from her spoon to delay her answer. "It was a spontaneous decision."

Minerva sighed and raked her hands through her dark hair extensions, lines beginning to crease around her mouth despite the recent bout of Botox she'd had. Clearly, Atlanta was aging her. She couldn't find it in her to feel guilty, though. She was an adult, now: an adult who had everything handed to her on a silver platter. What did her mother expect of her, when she had raised her that way?

"You know, I thought maybe the attack in London would have knocked some maturity into you."

"God, Mom, I went shopping in Paris and then came home. What's the problem?"

"The problem is that instead of waiting for things to blow over, you had to be the center of attention again." Minerva threw the magazine in front of Atlanta with a slap. The headline read *Atlanta Stone Spotted in Paris for First Time Since Hotel Armed Robbery*. Below, there was a blurry photograph of her sitting with Beck — nothing more than an indistinguishable figure in black beside an array of colorful shopping bags — by the Seine, and then an unflattering close-up of her battling through the pack of paparazzi, so blown up that she could make out even the faintest of hairs and blemishes on her face.

Atlanta rolled her eyes and pushed the magazine away. "I didn't ask to be swarmed by paps."

"But you must have expected it. You know by now that they're vultures. They'll find you anywhere."

"Well, so what?" Atlanta asked in exasperation. "What am I supposed to do? Never go anywhere again? I thought the whole point of hiring a bodyguard was so that I could keep living my life."

"But you're goading them, Atlanta!" Minerva's brittle voice rose in frustration. "Look at you, with all your shopping bags. You were just robbed, and it's as though you're flaunting that — as though you're asking for it to happen again."

Atlanta scoffed in disgust, dropping her spoon. It landed in her bowl with an ear-splitting clatter, yogurt and granola splattering across the pristine surface. Minerva barely flinched. "Are you kidding me? I didn't ask for this. I didn't ask for any of this."

Minerva closed her eyes, lips pressed into a thin line — or as thin as her lip fillers would allow. When she opened them again, they were cool, steady. "All I ask is that you keep out of the public eye for a while as a safety precaution. Miss Harris herself said there's a possibility the attackers might still see you as a target. Anything could have happened in Paris. You don't know what you're dealing with right now. None of us do."

"I'm not going to stop living my life because of this." The metal legs of Atlanta's stool scraped across the pearl-white tiles as she pushed away from the bar. "We're not even in the same country as them anymore."

"Right, criminals can't book plane tickets," Minerva snarled, massaging her temples. "I almost lost my husband, Atlanta. I almost lost *you*."

Atlanta tried to push down the knot in her chest that came with her mother's words. She had been close to death that night, and so had Weston, but it was easier not to think of it that way. It was easier to pretend. Sometimes it was just another role she played: the fucked-up actress held at gunpoint. It only felt real when Minerva said it aloud, or when she woke up screaming.

"I know." The words scratched like sandpaper. "But we're fine now."

Minerva's expression remained unconvinced, but her shoulders slumped in resignation. "Just be careful, all right? For me."

"Fine." Atlanta's agreement was empty of any commitment. How could she keep a low profile when she was photographed every time she so much as went through the Starbucks drive-through? She wouldn't stay holed up in this place, and couldn't even if she wanted to, with her work schedule looming over the brief bout of freedom she was currently enjoying.

"Thank you." Minerva brightened. Atlanta had certainly inherited the ability to put on a mask anytime she pleased from her mother. "Now, I had Sophie bring a few dresses for you yesterday. They're in your closet. Try them on before hair and makeup get here, please, so we know what to do with you."

Atlanta furrowed her eyebrows, trying to recall next week's schedule. As far as she could remember, she only had an audition and a day on set — and the gala she had organized for this weekend, but there was no way she had told her mother about that. "Dresses?"

"For tonight." Minerva's eyes widened. "Don't tell me you forgot your brother's birthday."

Atlanta *had* forgotten, and she was certain that her blank expression made that clear.

"Oh, for god's sakes, Atlanta. Did you at least get him a gift?"

"I *am* the gift." Despite her joke, the thought of having to go anywhere tonight felt like a stab to the stomach, but at least there would be alcohol — among other things. She would need it to get through a night of fake friends asking how she was and burying themselves up her ass for a few Instagram selfies, despite the fact that she hadn't heard from anybody once when she'd been in London. That combined with her parents praising the heavenly saint that was her brother as a way of shaming Atlanta's own behavior sounded like the worst possible way to spend her evening.

"You have ten different bags in this picture" — Minerva jabbed the magazine again — "and not one of them is a gift for Anderson?"

"That depends," she huffed, rubbing her eyes free of sleep. "Do you think Anderson would wear women's size eight Gucci loafers?"

At a loss, Minerva shook her head and checked the time on her iPhone. "Forget it. You shower, I'll have my assistant dash out for something."

"Ugh," Atlanta groaned and slouched, already padding out of the kitchen with labored steps. "I swear you just asked me to keep a low profile. I don't think a birthday party counts as discreet."

"It's your brother's birthday." Minerva waved her off, already flicking through the magazine again with fading interest. "Perhaps your gift to us all can be less complaining."

Atlanta fought the urge to hold up her middle finger in contempt, her stomach sinking as she left. There would be no getting out of this today.

* * *

Beck didn't like LA. Stepping off the plane had momentarily blinded her. The sun was a rare thing in England — especially in winter — and it would take some getting used to. Her corneas still hadn't adjusted to the eternal sheen that veiled everything here so that even the most mundane of things — asphalt, brick, tap water — seemed brighter, shinier, more colorful, as though she were skimming through pictures in a glossy magazine rather than living in them.

And she'd had to buy new clothes the first chance she'd gotten. There was no place for her thick jackets and sweaters here, not unless she wanted to be permanently soaked with sweat, so she had let Eric take her to one of the less glamorous malls nearby to pick out a few shirts after a quick meeting at WPG's LA headquarters.

The jet lag was killing her, too, so much so that she had to suppress a very guttural groan when Atlanta summoned her later in the afternoon. She had been snoozing in her makeshift office a few miles from the main house, where there were bedrooms for the staff and a desk of computers provided by the Stones.

The family house was as fancy as she had imagined, though not quite the grand manor they had rented in England. This was more modern and towered atop the high, dusty California hills. From the office, Beck followed the garden path around a large pool and a collection of sun lounges into a house of white stone and large windows. Inside the rooms were so vast that the house felt empty. No amount of furniture filled the hallways, and no family pictures hung on the walls the way Beck would have expected in a normal house. No, it was almost as though the house was furnished for the realtors to sell: a show house, with the icy draught of the air conditioning the only entity roaming the halls.

Atlanta's room was at the very end of a long corridor two stories up. Minerva had given Beck a quick tour upon her arrival, and that had been about the only information she'd retained in her jet-lagged state. She knocked on the door now, patiently.

"Come in," Atlanta called from within. Beck opened the door, stepped in, and immediately left again.

Atlanta had been in the middle of getting dressed, her golden skin bare as she shimmied into something shiny that Beck hadn't time to really look at. Thankfully, her back had been to the door, but still — was this another game? Was she *still* trying to fluster her?

It wasn't going to work.

Even if Beck's heart had sped up ever so slightly.

"I said come in," Atlanta repeated. Beck sighed through clenched teeth and obeyed, this time shutting the door behind her and maintaining as blank an expression as she could.

"I was told the party wasn't for another few hours, Miss Stone."

"It's not." Atlanta pulled on the straps of her

dress and gave herself a once-over in the mirror. The column of her spine was still exposed, curling as she moved in a way that Beck tried not to notice. "But I couldn't decide what dress to wear, and you're the only other woman under forty in the house besides my terribly dressed assistant. She turned up today in a pleated skirt, Beck. *A pleated skirt.*"

"Oh, no," Beck replied, keeping her voice monotone. She had never had the luxury herself to care about fashion faux pas. "Not a pleated skirt."

Atlanta turned around, putting the dress on full display. It was low-cut and high-hemmed, highlighting her slender torso and the narrow valley between her breasts, as well as her long legs. The color, though — Beck didn't like it, even if Atlanta was the type who could pull off anything. It was a bright blue, cool-toned, and too sparkly.

"Sorry," Atlanta apologized, a faint smirk uncoiling on her lips. "I hope this isn't inappropriate, Miss Harris."

The suggestive gravel in her tone told Beck that she hoped it was anything but. Beck flashed her a tight-lipped smile, as nonchalant as she could offer in the hopes of denting the woman's ego. "Nothing I haven't seen before, love."

"Oh, is that right?" Atlanta raised an eyebrow as though impressed, though Beck could see the disappointment dancing in her eyes. Beck doubted that Atlanta Stone was used to being shrugged off.

Beck hummed and crossed her arms, eyeing the other dresses laid out on the bed. "Do you want my advice, or were you just bored?"

"Both," she admitted.

Swallowing down a laugh, Beck said, "Then I'd go with the red one."

"All right." Atlanta shuffled out of the blue dress, displaying nothing but her lacy, almost non-existent underwear. Beck found a spot on the wall and burned a hole into it with her stare, knowing that a reaction was exactly what Atlanta wanted. The tops of her ears were beginning to burn. Thank god they were covered by her hair. "Red it is."

"Do you often change in front of your employees?" Beck asked the question as though she might be asking for the time: aloof, the answer inconsequential.

"Only my favorite ones." Atlanta grinned, pulling the red dress on without haste. Beck made a point of meeting her gaze as she slid the material up her legs to her hips and then her chest and shoulders. Atlanta flicked her blonde hair across one shoulder. "Zip me up?"

"Does this work often?" Beck obeyed, weaving behind Atlanta. She made sure to keep her fingers from brushing against Atlanta's skin, and zipped the dress up with careless haste so that she could step away as soon as her lower back was covered.

"Does what work often?" Atlanta brushed

her hair back so that it cascaded across her shoulders. The color did suit her better, the red offsetting the different strands of gold and warming the brown of her eyes.

"Your little flirting game."

The corner of Atlanta's mouth quivered. "I don't know what you mean, Miss Harris."

"If you say so." Beck swiped her tongue across her teeth, her eyes scanning the room curiously. It was slightly more interesting than the rest of the house, with movie posters and tapestries hanging across the walls and a chaise longue in the corner, piled with fluffy pillows. A typewriter sat — untouched, Beck would wager — by the dresser, and a large closet full of shoes and handbags had been left open beside the en suite. It wasn't quite as girly or showy as Beck had expected. In fact, minus the ridiculous collection of mirrors and clothes, it was cozy and almost… normal.

"You're right." Atlanta admired her figure in the mirror, smoothing down the dress. "Red is perfect. You've got surprisingly good taste."

Beck let the backhanded compliment slip past her. "Will that be all for now, Miss Stone?"

"No, actually. I wanted to ask what *you* will be wearing. Obviously it needs to be something that isn't too conspicuous."

"Why?" Beck quipped. "Want to color-coordinate?"

"I'm just saying there'll be a crowd there. You should blend in." Atlanta gathered up another one of the dresses on her bed — only Beck realized now that it wasn't a dress. It was the blazer Atlanta had bought in Paris. "Maybe you could wear this."

Beck huffed. "You don't give up, do you?"

Atlanta shrugged. "It's in your size. May as well take it." When Beck made no move to do such a thing, Atlanta's gaze turned cold. "You know, you're not fooling me with this whole superiority complex. Everybody wants to be rich and wear nice things. It's okay to admit that, Beck."

"Everybody wants to be rich," Beck answered stonily. "Nobody needs to be."

"It must be so easy to see the world in black and white." Atlanta took a step closer to her. Beck caught a sharp hint of peppermint on her breath. Even her bloody toothpaste smelled expensive.

"Yes, love, I'm the narrow-minded one." Beck scowled and snatched the blazer from her. "This won't be a habit. I'll wear the bloody thing, and then you'll back off."

"Beck Harris, forced to wear luxurious, stylish, and comfortable clothing. My heart bleeds for her," Atlanta gasped dramatically, pouting. "Get over yourself. It'll look good on you."

"Modesty would look good on you, love," Beck griped as she left, the material bunched in her fists. "But you probably couldn't afford it."

SEVEN

Atlanta's cheeks ached from forcing so many smiles. The music blasted loud enough through the speakers that her bones pulsed with it, and where usually she enjoyed losing herself in the cacophony of partying, drinking, dancing, now it only made her stomach churn with anxiety. Each time she weaved through the crowd, she imagined a gun pressed to her temple, remembered how it had felt to be intoxicated and unable to fight back. Each broad shoulder that nudged past her brought with it a wave of déjà vu so fierce she could barely breathe.

It seemed not to affect her family. While Atlanta chased down her champagne with vodka, and chased down vodka with martinis until her head felt fuzzy enough that she no longer had space to think about the nerves roiling in her stomach, her family mingled with celebrities and VIPs until their conversations merged into one unintelligible babble of nonsense. Anderson had made out with at least five women already, his collar stained with lipstick that he was now furiously trying to scrub off with a serviette at the bar before Minerva caught him and finally realized he was not the sweet little boy she had spoiled rotten as a child.

Beck stood by the pillars at the edge of the Stones' large kitchen, a sturdy brick wall against a tumultuous tempest of people. She watched her surroundings intently, an earpiece wire coiling into her collar. She wore the blazer Atlanta had bought in Paris, as requested, with a low-cut satin shirt and tailored trousers. Professional, but sleek enough that the material clung to the lean muscles of her legs. She had seemed so dainty the day they'd met, yet now Atlanta could see that her body was corded with strength. It was attractive, yes, but a comfort, too. She would be able to protect her if she had to. She had proven that in Paris.

Even so, Atlanta had chosen not to acknowledge her tonight, lest she see just how uneasy she was. She didn't want Beck — steadfast, brave, tough Beck — to think her weak or pathetic.

She didn't want to *feel* weak and pathetic.

A tall frame sat down on the couch beside her without permission, and Atlanta glanced at them just long enough to find Hugo Dean donning his usual smarmy smirk: her "ex," if she was generous enough to regard him as such. They'd had a brief fling designed for the cameras after starring in a television show together last year, when their on-screen romance was not enough for fans and they had to fake it off-screen, too. Now she could barely stand to be around him.

Especially when he smirked at her like that,

all perfect teeth and dimples.

"It's been a while, Lanta. How are you?"

"Peachy," Atlanta deadpanned, gulping down the last dregs of her martini and then snatching a glass of champagne from the waiter walking by. "I didn't realize you were coming tonight."

"Your brother and I are pretty tight, I guess." He shrugged haughtily.

Atlanta hummed doubtfully, eyeing the unending string of guests passing by. "Along with the rest of LA's general population, it seems."

"What's wrong, Lanta? Aren't you enjoying yourself?" Hugo leaned in close enough to whisper in her ear, his hand sliding up Atlanta's thigh. A signature Hugo Dean move, and Atlanta knew exactly what it meant: he was on the prowl, and she was his target. She had been happy about that, once, even when it meant choking on his pungent cologne and faking all of her orgasms in bed. Now it only made her nauseous. One of Atlanta's only rules was that she never crawled back to an ex. "Let me see if I can help with that."

Atlanta fought the urge to gag against the bubbles of champagne sliding down her throat. "No girlfriend tonight, Hugo?"

He paused when he reached the hem of her dress. "I don't have a girlfriend."

"No? Well, I sure hope the blonde you were making out with on your Instagram post wasn't your sister."

Hugo's blue eyes glittered in amusement, and he narrowed them into his perfect little smolder. "Have you been keeping tabs on me?"

Atlanta shrugged, her heel brushing against his calf. She might as well have her fun for a little while, since she had nothing better to do here. Besides, the alcohol was taking effect, and cocktails turned her into a shameless flirt — even more than she usually was. "Don't flatter yourself. I was bored in London. I had time to kill, and I was tagged in about ten different articles about it on Twitter."

"Is it true what they're saying?" His expression suddenly sobered, his thick eyebrows knitting together. "Did he try to kill you?"

Acid seared in her gut. She didn't want to talk about this. Her focus flitted past him, to a blur of figures. One blonde in particular stood out: the model she had seen in Hugo's picture, scrutinizing them both with a wicked, envious glint in her eye. "Your sister's waiting for you."

"I want you back," Hugo whispered at the same time, his hands finding hers. His touch wasn't soft, but demanding.

"Why?" Her words were becoming lazy. "Got a new show out you need to promote?"

"A movie, actually," he admitted with a dry grin. "But that's not the only reason. We were good together, weren't we, Lanta?"

Atlanta rolled her eyes and pulled herself away from him, her knee knocking against the glass coffee table and causing the drinks laid out in front of her to swish dangerously. "It wasn't real, Hugo. Get over it."

"Oh, come on, babe. Don't be like that." Hugo's wandering hands found the base of her spine and grazed her dress before inching lower.

Atlanta scoffed and stood before he could go too far, stumbling only slightly on her heels. She had plenty of practice acting sober when she was drunk, so much so that she might have been able to walk a tightrope under the influence at this point. "Not interested. Sorry."

"Atlanta." Hugo clamped her wrist and tried to drag her back down. She fought to prize herself from his grip, and was freed at the same time that she felt Beck's reassuring presence behind her.

"Is there a problem, Miss Stone?" Her question was thick with warning, eyes shooting razor-sharp daggers toward Hugo. Her protectiveness caused something deep in Atlanta's belly to stir, much more pleasant and warm than the nausea she had felt before, with Hugo.

"Who the hell are you?" Hugo rose to tower over Beck. Atlanta would still bet on her if they came to blows, though, with the amount of venom blazing from her. That matched with the fact that she was wearing pointed heels that could easily penetrate flesh would guarantee her the winner.

Atlanta imagined how gratifying it would be to see Beck destroy a six-foot-three cocky bastard like Hugo.

"She's my bodyguard," Atlanta said finally. "So if I were you, I'd keep my hands to myself — unless you want her to cut them off."

Hugo looked Beck up and down in disbelief, itching at his well-trimmed stubble. "Jesus, do they hire anyone these days?"

"Rest assured, Mr. Dean" — Beck flashed a saccharine smile as she spoke — "I'm quite competent at my job. Atlanta?"

Atlanta fired Hugo a final scowl before she ambled off, weaving through a thousand different sequinned dresses and collared shirts until she reached the bar. Beck loitered just behind as she ordered four more shots and downed them all, uncaring if her mother found her. If she was going to get through the rest of the night, she needed to be drunk.

When she was done, she caught sight of the outdoor pool glittering beyond the patio doors. Fresh air: that was what she needed.

Fresh air, and about ten more shots of vodka, probably.

* * *

Beck could have stopped at the patio doors if she'd wanted to. She didn't have to go outside after Atlanta, since the grounds and neighborhood were secure. And yet, without stopping to think about it, she followed her through the doors.

Atlanta stumbled by the edge of the pool,

unsteady enough that Beck sped up in fear that she was about to fall in. By the time she had grabbed her by the arms to prop her up, she realized that Atlanta was only slipping off her high heels.

"Going for a swim, love?"

"Why? Wanna skinny-dip?" A mangled sound that might have been a laugh caught in Atlanta's throat as she tossed her stilettos aside and sat. The pool water lapped around her ankles, manicured, blistered toes wiggling in the black. The lights from the house danced against the still water, but with the doors closed, the night blanketed them in a welcome silence.

Beck couldn't help but scrutinize Atlanta closely as she swished her feet. She looked as she had that night in Paris. Solemn. Alone. Beck had seen her falter earlier only because she was looking closely enough. While everyone else laughed and chattered and took photographs, Atlanta drank. Perhaps the attack had affected her more than Beck had initially thought. Or perhaps this life was not as easy as everybody made it seem. Either way, her eyes were glassy and hooded, her body swaying even when she was seated.

"What time is it, Beck?" Atlanta's words slurred together. She let out a long breath, ragged with exhaustion.

Beck pulled back her sleeves to check her wristwatch. "Almost one."

Atlanta's response was a groan, and she tilted her head back as though in prayer. Her perfect curls collapsed from her face, chest swelling as she sucked in the fresh air.

"Would you like me to escort you to your room, Miss Stone?" Beck questioned carefully as Atlanta straightened, their eyes finally meeting. Even exhausted and drunk, she was striking, her golden hair spilling across her shoulders and her lips painted a deep shade of red that matched the dress. Everybody had fawned over her beauty earlier on. Beck wondered what that must feel like. Her own job was to be unnoticeable, to blend in, and she did it well. She had never felt the weight of a thousand different eyes on her — and would never want to.

"The jacket looks good on you" was all Atlanta said, a lazy smile uncoiling itself. Her eyes roamed Beck not for the first time tonight. Beck didn't shy from them. She had known that Atlanta would find pleasure in the low-cut shirt she wore, had chosen it anyway. It wasn't often she got to look pretty. Tonight she had made the most of the opportunity.

She didn't quite know why.

Beck lowered herself beside Atlanta finally, freeing her tender feet from their heels and turning up her trousers at the ankle. The cool water was soothing, welcome. She pressed her lips together, glad when she was freed from Atlanta's gaze, and leaned back on her hands. "Thank you."

"You didn't have to help me with Hugo."

"It's my job," Beck responded curtly, though

she knew it wasn't. Atlanta was probably used to slimy men like him pining for her and groping her, and she was certain she could handle herself. Still, Beck had intervened without thinking. Seeing men like him thinking they had a right to touch women, to make them cringe away... it knocked her sick.

"To protect me from gross exes?" Atlanta raised an eyebrow in amusement. "I might keep you around for a while, then. I have plenty."

"I don't doubt it." For once, Beck kept the judgment from her words. "Are you okay, Atlanta?"

The question was enough to earn a glimpse of surprise from Atlanta. Her eyes swam with something indecipherable — something painful. In response, an aching feeling welled in Beck: a need to protect her from whatever it was, perhaps. Because it was her job. Because...

Because. For all Atlanta's flaws — and there were plenty — Beck saw something in her she hadn't been expecting. Only flashes, in the crumbling gaps in the barrier she kept solidly around her, but enough. This wasn't a spoiled brat getting drunk because she had nothing better to do. Something was bothering her tonight. She was struggling.

And then Beck remembered whom she was dealing with. She remembered the shopping trip, and the incessant flirting because Atlanta was used to having everybody wrapped around her finger, and she felt ridiculous for even caring. Atlanta

Stone would be just fine. Atlanta Stone didn't need pity or friendship.

Atlanta Stone needed Beck to do her job, and that was it.

"Fine," Atlanta said evasively. "You know, you haven't called me 'love' tonight."

"Haven't I?" Beck smirked. In truth, she had been trying to be more professional, especially since they were in such a public setting. The way she'd been with Atlanta... it wasn't how she usually was. She had developed friendships with a few of her clients before, but had never bickered with them or teased them so openly. She had never let them goad her or play games. She knew she could get away with it when they were alone, and it worked fine enough that way, but nobody else would understand it. The last thing she needed was Minerva to overhear and fire her. "Does that bother you?"

Atlanta shrugged. "Maybe."

Beck laughed it off and turned, eyeing the guests through the glass doors. This world was miles away from the one she had grown up in. She sometimes caught herself wondering why she was still here, working for entitled snobs she didn't even like. But what was the alternative? She could think of none.

"What do you see when you look at us, Beck?" Atlanta studied her intently, features still drooping with intoxication.

"Who's 'us'?"

"Them. Me. My family."

The moment felt too peaceful, too intense, to break it with sarcasm or honesty. Beck loosed a breath, scraping her fingers through her air. "I don't know. I see what I see in everyone, I suppose. People who are lost, and just trying to find their place."

"You loathe us." Atlanta dragged out her *O* so that it came out like a song.

"Because I've seen the other side of it. I've seen people with no money, no job, no nothing. To watch you spray thousands of dollars' worth of champagne around the house for minimum-wage cleaners to take care of tomorrow… it doesn't sit right."

"But if you hate it so much, why do you protect us?" she asked. "You could be anywhere, Beck. Why are you here?"

Beck hesitated. She had wondered that herself more than enough times. She kicked her feet out, water splashing her trousers. "Maybe I'm a little bit lost, too."

Her resolve hardened at the echo of her own words. She didn't want this. She didn't want to open up, especially not to her client and especially not when that client was drunk. She cleared her throat and straightened out her jacket, professional again.

"Would you like me to escort you to your room, Miss Stone?" she repeated.

Resignedly, Atlanta slumped and nodded,

exhaustion tugging at her features. "Yes." It came out as a whispered, hoarse plea that scraped against Beck's heart. "Yes, please."

EIGHT

Atlanta waltzed into the office surprisingly early the next day. Beck lifted her head from the computer, where she had been searching for any hints of criminals or syndicates who might have been in London the night of the armed robbery. Still no luck, not with only Atlanta's vague description to go off of.

She closed the tab as the door swung shut, her chin placed wearily in her hand as she swiveled toward the actress. "I didn't think you'd be up yet."

If Atlanta were embarrassed for the state she'd been in last night, she didn't show it. Instead she wore her usual smug expression, a notebook in one hand and her phone in the other. "I wanted to clear my schedule with you. The copy you got from my mother isn't correct."

"Oh?"

Atlanta perched on the edge of Beck's desk, her hair spilling across her shoulders like molten gold. Beck thanked the gods that her coworkers were off with their own duties and weren't here to witness whatever barbed conversation they were about to have. "I have a charity gala at the Beverly Hilton tomorrow. I planned it myself, and my mother knows nothing about it. I'd prefer to keep it that way."

"Okay." Beck sucked in a breath at the thought of having to conceal any information from Minerva, but brought up her itinerary on her computer and found tomorrow's date. "When will you need me?"

"All day, from around ten." Atlanta clicked her pen incessantly as she scanned over a page in her notebook. "I have a hair appointment in the morning, and then a facial, nails, Brazilian" — her mouth quirked up at that, eyes glancing pointedly at Beck — "before I collect my dress, have my stylists make me even more beautiful than usual, and then we'll be heading to walk the carpet at around six."

Beck typed furiously to keep up with her words, brows furrowed in concentration. "Got it. I assume the event will have a large number of attendees?"

"Around three hundred," Atlanta replied. "Not too many. But there'll be plenty of paps and fans outside."

Beck wanted to balk at Atlanta's idea of "not too many." Instead she reclined in her chair and chewed on the end of her pen. "In that case, I'll have some extra security come out and make a plan with the venue. Anything else?"

"Nope. That's all." Atlanta slapped her notebook shut with a dry grin. "The dress code is formal, so wear something pretty for me."

"I always do, don't I?" The coy remark fell from Beck's lips without thought, and there was no taking it back. She cleared her throat and stood, heading into the small kitchen to pour herself another mug of coffee so that she wouldn't have to wait for her words to resonate. "Should I prepare for any more groping ex-boyfriends?"

"Ex-boyfriends, no." Atlanta followed her in, slouching against the doorframe. Beck didn't bother to ask if she wanted coffee, instead sipping and wincing at the foul taste. She'd forgotten milk, and she missed the earthy comfort of her Yorkshire tea. "Ex-girlfriends, on the other hand..."

Internally, Beck rolled her eyes. Another way of getting a reaction, or was she trying to impress Beck? Beck wouldn't give her the satisfaction of either. "I'll keep it in mind. What's the charity?"

"There are a few, actually." Atlanta worried at her lip, everything about her seeming to shift in an instant. She took this seriously... Beck never thought she'd see the day, but somehow, it had come. Atlanta Stone did care about something, after all. "All women's charities. Some that focus on issues in other countries and continents, some on minority groups, and a few for domestic abuse, sexual assault survivors, and Planned Parenthood."

Beck raised her eyebrows, stunned. "And you organized it all?"

Atlanta seemed to draw pleasure from the reaction. She grinned, patting Beck on the shoulder before she made to leave. "Don't act so surprised, Beck. It's insulting."

"I suppose I just didn't realize that Atlanta Stone had a heart." It was a lie: she had realized last night, and before that, in Paris, that perhaps there was more to the actress than her whitened teeth and her bank account. She just hadn't been expecting something as big as this. For a cause that mattered.

A cause that mattered to Beck, no less.

Atlanta came to a stop by the door and winced dramatically — her mask was back, and it overwhelmed the entire room with its insincere grin. "It was a shock for me, too, Miss Harris. Don't get used to it, though."

Beck shook her head. "I wouldn't dream of it," she muttered to herself as the door of the office slammed shut behind Atlanta.

NINE

Atlanta focused on the sunset dripping through the palm trees to distract herself from the mercilessness of the flashing lights. Anxiety swelled in her stomach as she emerged from her limousine, straightening out her silver dress before the cameras could catch her all awry. Her personal assistant, Sophie, came out next, linking her arm through hers, and she was glad at least for some support.

It had never affected her like this before. She had always been so calm and confident, playing up for her enraptured audience and enjoying every slither of attention she'd ever gotten. Now she could think only of the hotel room, and the gun, and see only shadowed figures lurking behind the line of paparazzi. Both that and the fact that this was the first event she had planned and attended that actually *mattered* and therefore had to be perfect weighed on her chest and made it difficult to so much as blink.

Beck followed last, and Atlanta glanced at her warily. Something in her eyes must have given her away, because Beck offered her a tight, reassuring smile and a nod. Her face was painted in warm, shimmering colors tonight, with smoky eyes that made the ring of green around her pupils glow and a deep, silky mauve lipstick. With her dark hair curling across her square face, she was all captivating darkness, the type of beauty that Beck probably didn't even recognize in herself with her constant focus on work. More beautiful than Atlanta had ever seen her. Quickly, Atlanta stored away any vulnerability she might have been showing, her eyes shuttering as she lifted her chin in the direction of the crowd. They cheered for her, and in return, she offered them one of her winning smiles with an elegant wave.

Sophie urged Atlanta forward, toward them. She posed for the photographers, signed autographs, laughed when she was supposed to, all in a stomach-churning, head-spinning, heart-racing daze.

"Atlanta," a woman holding a microphone called in front of her. As she shielded her eyes from the lights, Atlanta recognized her from an interview she'd done a few years back. E! News, if Atlanta remembered rightly. Her name was lost on her tongue, though. "How are you feeling after the attack in London? Is it true that you were held at gunpoint?"

The stone in Atlanta's stomach sank painfully lower, until it was all she could focus on as the microphone fell to her. She scanned the crowd behind her. Beck still stood not too far away, spine as straight as ever and eyes cast intently on Atlanta. She wore a low-cut blouse with wide-legged trousers that whispered together each time she walked. Atlanta had shamelessly ogled her earlier tonight before veiling a compliment with sarcasm.

Her thoughts of her bodyguard had dragged Atlanta away from the interview, and when their gazes met across the golden walkway, she snapped her attention back to the presenter. She could only whittle off a torrent of bullshit about how the attack had only made the family stronger and how they were healing both mentally and physically, as Sophie had forced her to rehearse over and over on the ride here. She was glad when she was moved on to the next interviewer, and the next, until her words were clipped and wooden and her throat dry and cracked.

It took every fiber of her being to stay on the carpet, with only a rope separating her from frenzied press and fans. Every instinct in her told her to run. Every step she took, she imagined coming face-to-face with a gun the way she had in the hotel that night.

She hoped to god they were serving something stronger than champagne tonight.

✻ ✻ ✻

Beck did not see how partying in a high-ceilinged ballroom with chandeliers hanging overhead did anything to help victims of assault. She did not see how Atlanta stuffing herself with salmon puffs and olives and guzzling down alcohol would mend the traumas endured by women all over the world. Atlanta seemed to think that she was doing a good thing, and as predicted, she had prattled something predictable and very clearly scripted onstage about how important this event was, and how everybody *must* donate.

There were surely better ways of helping.

Still, Beck did her job. She trailed Atlanta while she socialized, noticing the exact moment when the champagne took its toll and she grew drowsy and giggly. She watched her pretend to listen to other women's stories, Beck's own heart aching for them more than Atlanta's no doubt ever would. She escorted her to the bathroom and put up with her stupid little games while Atlanta re-applied her Chanel lipstick, blotting it on a tissue before pressing it to Beck's cheek.

She would admit that the founders of the charities themselves left an impact with their own speeches. Many women went onstage to share their horrendous experiences, all of them causing a lump to gather in Beck's throat. So many. There were so many who had felt helpless, who had been made small, like her mother.

It was exactly why Beck had chosen this. *These* were the people she had wanted to protect when she had decided this future for herself. Instead she was stuck with a shallow actress who understood nothing of these struggles.

And even if she did, what good would this

do? They were only raising awareness among other women, rather than holding the perpetrators accountable and preventing it from happening again.

Beck wanted more than anything to leave, but the only small gift she was given was when Atlanta sauntered off onto the balcony after her sixth flute of champagne. Like the night at the party, Beck could have remained stationed by the doors, but she needed the fresh air far more than Atlanta.

Atlanta braced herself against the railings, her eyes hooded as she looked out onto the city. Beck mirrored her wordlessly. At night, LA didn't seem so different from London, or Beck's home city, Manchester. The palm trees were mere silhouettes, the roads indistinguishable from any other as a line of traffic waited for the red lights to change below. The honking of horns sounded just the same. The only things that served as a reminder of where she was were the Hollywood sign high in the hills across the way and the warm breeze that carried Atlanta's lavish perfume. For a moment, and for the first time in a long time, Beck wondered about her family.

"Are you having fun?" Atlanta questioned finally without looking at her.

"Oh, yeah, a blast." The barbs sharpening Beck's words couldn't be blunted. She was bristling with them.

By the way that Atlanta faltered, Beck could tell it wasn't the reaction she'd been expecting.

"You've been walking around all pouty and brooding all night — even more than usual. Have I done something to offend you, Beck?"

"Nothing at all, Miss Stone." Beck's lips spread into a thin smile, head cocked to one side.

Lines creased Atlanta's forehead. God, Beck hated this. She hated working for people so far removed from her own world. With businesspeople, it wasn't so bad. Some of them were arrogant and had inherited their wealth without a day of real work, yes, but others had built their empire from nothing.

If she were to be rational, she could admit that the subject matter tonight had only added fuel to her fire. It had reminded her of her family, her mother, resurfacing feelings and memories she would rather forget. It had reminded her of the horrors she had witnessed in the army. But she didn't feel like being rational anymore, so she only glared at the stars and prayed for this nightmare to be done with so that she could go home.

"I thought..." Atlanta stumbled over her words — whether from champagne or surprise, Beck didn't know. "I thought you'd be impressed. You were so certain I was vapid and superficial."

Beck's harsh laugh cleaved the static air in two. "Was this supposed to change my mind, love?"

"All night, you've listened to these women's stories, and you're telling me that it doesn't matter?" Atlanta's voice crackled with frustration.

"I'm not saying that. In fact, I haven't said anything. You jumped to that conclusion all on your own."

"But you're looking at me like I just pissed in your champagne." Her throat bobbed as she swallowed. Her cheeks had flushed with color, fingers trembling against the railing. Beck knew why *she* was angry, but why on earth was Atlanta? "Why?"

Beck shook her head, gathering her composure with a long breath. "Does it matter what I think?"

"Yes!" Atlanta shouted, so loudly that it overpowered the classical music coming from within.

Beck's eyes narrowed in challenge. "Why?"

Atlanta's mouth opened. Shut. Nothing came out but a ragged expulsion of air, diamond earrings rocking and tangling with her hair. "I don't know," she whispered finally. "It just does."

Beck sniffed, clutching the railing with so much force that it might have snapped in her hands. A breeze curled through her hair. It was so rare that she left it down, especially when she was working, but she had made an effort tonight. She had no idea why. "I just think," she murmured steadily, finally, "that there are better ways to help than a fancy gala with an open bar."

"It's the best way to get sizable donations."

"And how many of those sizable donations are halved because of the price they paid for their dress or their hair stylist?" Beck asked. "Do the people in there even check to see the difference it makes? Do they *care*, or do they just have money to burn while they get their pictures taken and live it up with other celebrities? There are women out there with nothing, Atlanta. *Nothing*. And while raising awareness and having people donate might make some kind of impact, what good does it do those who are forgotten? Those who not even *your* money can reach?"

Atlanta's chin wobbled. She brushed the hair from her face, blinking. "I can't change the world, Beck. I can only do what I can."

"And what is that? Buy ten-thousand-dollar handbags from designer shops and drink yourself into oblivion?"

"Why does it bother you so much?"

"Why *doesn't* it bother you?" Beck retaliated, biting down on the inside of her cheek, desperate to make her see. Why couldn't she just *see*?

"I thought I was doing something good." Atlanta's voice broke so devastatingly that Beck's heart halted. It drew the anger from her, snuffed out the fire, and left her feeling raw and hollow and charred. This wasn't her job and it wasn't her place, and she couldn't blame Atlanta for all of the wrong in the world, no matter how angry it made her.

Beck closed her eyes against the breeze, tucking her chin as she inhaled again, searching. For patience. For understanding. For peace. "You are." The admission was strained; she wasn't sure how much she believed it. "But if you really want to help, Atlanta, it's going to take more than a fancy gala."

More silence. Beck didn't want to fill it, hoped, foolishly perhaps, that her words were sinking in.

"You're right," Atlanta said finally. "I know that you are. I just… I've never seen the bad parts of life. I mean, I've had a few slimy directors, but I was lucky enough to have ways out. I was never desperate enough for a role, or for a paycheck, and I never got trapped. I've always lived in a big house, always been comfortable and wealthy and able to buy anything I want. I've never known it any other way. I can't even imagine going through the things those women talked about. Most of the time, I pretend it doesn't happen at all."

It made sense, then, that she couldn't see past the excess. Beck softened slightly, but Atlanta continued.

"It's made me messy and ignorant and stupid. I know that, too. But it's easier to be those things. Everybody thinks they have a right into my personal life. In return, I give them what they want: a mess with too much money. A joke. An airhead who happens to be a mediocre actress. Because the alternative is to try to be real, vulnerable, in a world that breaks those types of people, and how can I let myself?

"I give them what they expect of me. I use

it as a shield. Somehow, along the way, it stopped being an act. Everything, every part of me, became a performance." A humorless chuckle that tore Beck in two. "You're the only person who's ever called me out on it."

Beck didn't know what to say. There was no cheap taunt or blunt accusation left to be given. Everything she had ever judged Atlanta on — it made sense now. Beck was so passionate about her views because she had been born into nothing at all. Atlanta had been born into everything. She had never had to know those struggles. She only had to protect herself from a poisonous industry that thrived on other people's suffering. It was no wonder they were so different.

"You're not the problem," Beck said with a rare tenderness in her tone. "You're just a small part of it."

Her hair whipped across her face, and she made no move to tear it away. Instead she fixed her gaze on the Hollywood sign and let the truth spill out of her for the first time.

"I grew up poor. My family and I... we didn't have much. My mum had to go through a lot of things those women talked about in there, and as soon as I was old enough, all I wanted was to protect her from it."

"Beck —" Atlanta breathed, tears rolling down her cheeks as she turned.

Beck couldn't look at her. She could do nothing but curl her fingers into her palms until her nails buried into her flesh. "I couldn't. I couldn't protect her, Atlanta. I was too small, and we had nothing — no help, no friends, no support. That's why I am this way. Because this gala… it would have made no difference to her. It's not your fault. I know that. But it still makes me —" She choked on the rest of her words, bowing her head, hating herself. She had never talked about this. Never. It made her feel weak and stupid and wrong.

But Atlanta didn't laugh, or scoff, or walk away. Her dark eyes swam with guilt, with sorrow, and she reached out slowly, probably waiting for Beck to snarl. Beck didn't.

Atlanta's fingers grazed Beck's, and she laced them together. Soft. Warm. Able to make her crumble, if she let them.

She wouldn't.

"I'm sorry." Beck could tell that Atlanta meant it: it flooded every syllable, every letter, until Beck had to bite down on her lip to stop it from trembling. She wouldn't cry. She would draw the line at that. "I'm so sorry."

Beck drew her hand away, straightened. Ever the soldier. Ever the guard. "You should go back inside, see to your guests."

"Beck…"

But Beck had nothing else to say — nothing that she *could* say, at least, so she opened the doors, the flimsy silk curtain rippling across her like a veil, and followed Atlanta back into the chandelier-lit ballroom. Pushing down any other emotions still threatening to resurface had become easy — so easy that she did it now in an instant.

Atlanta looked at her with regret only once before she pasted that beaming grin across her face again.

TEN

Strips of light crossed Beck's face as they made their way home, only an empty seat separating them. Between that and the gentle hum of the engine, Atlanta was ready for dozing off. She'd had too much to drink: she had realized that when the night air hit her on the way out, and Beck had had to keep her hand placed on the small of her back in case she stumbled.

She'd had to pretend her touch didn't cause warmth to blossom in her — no mean feat when she was drunk, especially since she was usually the type to babble about anything that popped into her head under the influence.

Tonight, though, with the weight of Beck's words pressing down on her and mingling with a guilt she'd never acknowledged before, she had skipped that merry stage and gone straight to sleepy, until it was an effort to keep her heavy lids open. She was aware of Beck watching her when she thought she wasn't looking, and forced herself upright if only for her benefit.

What a mess she must have looked to her.

Because you are, another voice niggled at the back of her mind. *Always have been. Everybody knows it, including Beck.*

She took in a deep breath and forced her spine up straighter against the leather seats, rearranging her dress so that the slit in the taffeta showed a little less of her shiny, golden thigh. She opened her mouth to say something — another apology, maybe, or questions about Beck's past that now floated in her mind — but was stopped before she could even muster the first syllable.

"Turn right on the next corner, Sid," Beck instructed Atlanta's chauffeur, shooting up and clutching the headrest of the passenger seat. An eerie green glow swam across her neck from the dashboard lights as she snapped her head back, eyes narrowing on whatever it was she saw.

Atlanta's heart began to hammer, stomach swirling with sudden dread.

"But the Stone residence is straight ahead, ma'am," Sid argued, eyebrows flicking up in the rearview mirror. A brave man, if he thought he could undermine Beck — especially when she looked and sounded as urgent and grave as she did now.

Beck's jaw clenched so tightly Atlanta could imagine her molars gnashing together. "I think we're being tailed," she said. "Turn right."

Her demand left no room for questioning. Wisely, Sid steered the wheel with his gloved hands, leather chafing against leather, as Beck watched through the side mirror. Atlanta gulped down her panic. "Who is it?"

Beck ignored her question. She was somewhere, now, where Atlanta couldn't reach. Her shoulders had squared, her fingers biting into her thigh. She cursed, and Atlanta craned her neck to look.

It was true: a black SUV was following, but it was impossible to get a glimpse of the driver with the headlights blinding them.

Atlanta imagined *him* sitting behind the wheel anyway, a gun in his hand. Every hair on her body rose in terror, staving off the intoxication that had been dizzying her a moment ago.

"Turn right again at the next chance you get," Beck said. "And then speed up."

"Yes, ma'am," Sid replied, and then they were swerving across the next corner so quickly that Atlanta had to cling onto her seatbelt for support.

"Is it them?" she asked weakly, eyes wide in fear.

"I don't know," Beck murmured. "Maybe." As she said it, she slid her revolver from its holster and clicked off the safety. Atlanta couldn't look at the black, gleaming metal. She could do nothing but clutch onto anything she could find and let Sid sling her about as they turned again under Beck's orders.

She dared a glance backward and saw the SUV still there, closer now than it had been. They were on an open road, only a gas station illuminating the night before they rolled by the less glamorous houses, apartments, and shops of LA.

"As fast as you can go, Sid."

"Doing my best, ma'am." The concentration turned Sid's voice taut.

"Atlanta, when I tell you to get down, I need you to do it, okay?" Beck's voice was steady, unafraid. How many times had she done this before? Held the weight of that gun as though it meant nothing?

Who was she?

Atlanta stuttered out her "Okay," fingers trembling as they searched desperately for something — *anything* — to keep her here, grounded, safe.

There was no time to find it.

She was thrown forward as the bumper of the car behind them collided with the rear of their own. She clamped her mouth shut to suppress a scream, Beck's shouts — "Down, Atlanta. Down!" — flooding her ears and overpowering anything else she might have heard, felt, seen. The seatbelt fought against her, tightening across her chest as she sank into her seat, shielded by the cushions.

Beck jabbed at the controls to roll down the window on her side, and then a rattle of gunshots rent the world apart until all that remained were white dots dancing across Atlanta's vision. The car was slammed forward again, this time with more force, and Beck answered the violent question with more shots.

A final thrust forward, accompanied by the

earsplitting grind of metal against metal, stole the wind from Atlanta, and she couldn't pull it back as they swerved, her stomach swooping with the velocity of it.

It halted so swiftly that Atlanta's brain shuddered in her skull and her neck twisted against the collision. This time it wasn't from the back, though. It was the front.

Atlanta's breath fell out of her in ragged bursts, her chest heaving with silent sobs as the glass of the windshield shattered onto Sid, onto her.

When her body adjusted to the fact that they were no longer moving, she looked to Beck desperately and winced against the twinge that shot through her neck in response.

"Are you okay?" Beck was unclipping her seatbelt faster than Atlanta could so much as whisper out a reply, eyes scanning Atlanta frantically before she peered out of the back window.

"I think so."

"Sid?" Beck asked. "Are you still with me?"

"Just about, ma'am," Sid hissed out. Atlanta looked to the side mirror and found a bloody gash blossoming by his graying eyebrows. The sight caused sour bile to rise in her throat. Her own face stung, and beads of red oozed from a few slices on Beck's face, too. The glass had caught them all.

That wasn't what Atlanta was most concerned about, though, and neither was Beck.

She unclipped her seatbelt, still poised with

the gun in her hands. Atlanta couldn't fathom how the woman didn't need even a second to breathe. Still, she followed her focus, breath hitching in her throat. The black SUV had crashed, too, the bumper curled around a signpost between lanes and the tires flat. Smoke snaked out of the front, but other than that, Atlanta caught no movement, no shadows, no nothing. The road was dead.

"Sid, can you get out of the car?" Beck questioned. It was answered by a click of his seatbelt and a curdling groan of pain.

"By crawling into the back, perhaps."

"Do it. Now." Beck was a coiled spring ready to leap, her knuckles sharp juts of white as she gripped the gun without taking her eyes off the SUV.

Atlanta slid across the seat to make room for Sid as he clambered his way into the back with them.

"I assume you know how to use a gun." Beck unleashed a hidden pistol from her belt and shoved it into Sid's hands before he could stammer out a reply. "I'm going to go over there. I want you to crawl out of the other side with Atlanta, keep low, and hide in the first safe place you find. Do you understand?"

"No!" Atlanta interjected as she fought her way out of her own seatbelt. "Beck, it's not safe. We need to get out of here. All of us."

Beck was already reloading her gun, face carved into complete determination. Nothing else lived there — no anger or fear, no concern whatsoever. She was a soldier of stone, cold and unrelenting. Atlanta didn't know if it was comforting or terrifying.

"I need to find them." Beck's muddy eyes flashed to Atlanta, locking her in place. Empty. They were so empty, and so hardened, that Atlanta didn't recognize her at all. "When I tell you to go, you go."

"Beck —"

"*Go.*"

Atlanta had no intention of listening — but Sid did. He worked around her to open Atlanta's door and they just about tumbled onto the concrete as one. At the same time, Beck emerged from the other side, the dented metal door swinging on its hinges. She paused for only a moment, a black figure sacrificing herself to the shadows as Sid urged Atlanta in the opposite direction, keeping her head ducked down with his hand. She inched only a few steps backward at a time, always watching. Waiting.

But when Beck reached the mangled SUV, it was clear the driver wasn't there. She checked both sides, disappearing behind the smoke. Atlanta watched in a crouch at the mouth of the nearest alley, senses flooded by the dank smell of garbage that had been left in the heat all day. *Come back now*, she pleaded with Beck silently. *Come back.* She didn't know if it was for her own safety or for Beck's, but not having her here while blood trickled across her face and Sid's body pressed into her own behind — it wasn't right. She was afraid. Afraid of who lurked. Afraid for Beck. Afraid for herself.

It only wrenched at her entire being when Beck climbed into the driver's seat of the smoking SUV. "No," she breathed, fighting against Sid's grip. "No, it's going to blow. Let me go."

"She knows what she's doing, Miss Stone." His clutch was unbreakable. Though in his fifties now, he was still taller and stronger than Atlanta, and his hands were iron shackles around her arms.

The smoke blackened as Beck's silhouette continued to dance through the windshield, until the engine spat out billowing shadows into the sky.

"Beck!" Atlanta screamed, no longer caring if the driver — her attacker — was still around to hear her. "Beck, get out!"

Finally Beck appeared again, setting off into a run as she looked over her shoulder at the wreckage. Just in time, too: the car burst into fragments a moment after, wreathing Beck's retreating figure with its bright orange flames.

ELEVEN

The only thing that Beck had retrieved from the SUV was a business card for a car-rental company — the same company she and her colleagues had rented their own vehicles from in LA.

A coincidence, probably, but it might give her some advantage when she looked into it properly tomorrow. Either way, it hadn't been worth nearly having her hair singed off for.

She tapped the card against the kitchen island now, lost in thought. Atlanta sat opposite, picking at a loose piece of skin on her thumb. She hadn't uttered a word since they'd walked through the door of the Stone house, but Beck could see all that she hadn't yet expressed seething from her like water coming to a boil — the fear, the panic, the anger at Beck. Perhaps Beck *had* been reckless to go to that car when her place was supposed to be by Atlanta's side... but how could she just let the driver go after he had almost killed them?

The infuriating actress had refused to see a doctor, so Beck sighed finally and dampened a cloth beneath the tap before putting it on the counter between them. Her skin was marred by pink scratches, her hair disheveled, and her silver dress ripped from the lacy hem to her mid-thigh. Beck had never seen her so out of sorts, and it made her ache with guilt. She should have done more. She should have stopped this before it had started.

"You should drink something hot. Coffee? Tea?"

Atlanta wrinkled her nose. "So British of you to assume we have tea in this house."

"So appalling of you that you don't," Beck countered, already searching the kitchen for a kettle. There was none: only a fancy coffee machine Beck hadn't an inkling how to use. "On second thought, you make the coffee."

She swallowed and shifted, unable to keep still with the adrenaline still pulsing through her — adrenaline, and frustration, grating on her insides. He was still out there. Maybe he had returned after they'd left. Maybe she could find him if she went back.

Scraping her hair back, Beck straightened out her jacket and put her gun back in its holster at her hip. "I need to go. I need to find him."

"The cops are already looking." It was true: they had given a quick statement not too long ago. It had given them a small intermission between the periods of silence that had passed since they'd gotten home. The rest of the Stone family were out doing whatever it was that rich, famous people did, and Beck had already called Phil and Eric and asked that their security be stepped up for the rest of the night.

"I can help them."

Atlanta stood, stool legs scraping against the floor as she gripped Beck's wrist. Despite the firmness of it, her fingers trembled against the inside of Beck's arm. It only made Beck more desperate to seek the person who had done this — to hunt the source of Atlanta's fear down and conquer it. "You're not going back out there."

"I told the neighborhood security to be extra vigilant tonight. You'll be fine here."

"You're not leaving me alone in the house when somebody is trying to kill me, Beck!" Atlanta's words were raw with panic. "It's your job to stay with me."

"It's my job to make you safe again." Beck fought to keep her voice steady, peeling Atlanta's fingers from her flesh gently. "I can't do that when he's still out there."

"You can't do it if you're not here, either. I'm your client. I'm ordering that you stay."

Beck could have reminded her that Minerva was her employer, not Atlanta. She could have argued her case again and again. Instead she took one look at Atlanta's glassy eyes, cold with shock and sunken with exhaustion, and she knew she couldn't. She couldn't leave her, alone and afraid. She would just have to endure the relentless tug to find the driver until tomorrow.

"Okay." Beck relaxed, pressing her palms forcefully against the rough edge of the counter.

Atlanta sank back onto her stool, eyes cast down so that Beck could see every shimmering smudge of eye shadow and smeared mascara on her lids. "I'll stay."

"Do you think it's the same men?" Atlanta's voice was small, like a child asking to be read a bedtime story.

"Probably. Either that, or you have a lot of enemies. I can't imagine why." Beck sighed despite her taunt, collapsing her weight back onto the stool. "If it is the same people, it means they're hell-bent on silencing you... enough to follow you all the way to LA."

Atlanta wrung out the damp cloth before dabbing it across her forehead, where a few trickles of blood had dried. "Yeah, I think they made that pretty clear."

"I have two theories." Beck was brainstorming aloud now, but she didn't care, couldn't see past the black haze and the way her body still thrummed like a war drum. "We're either dealing with some type of syndicate, or your attacker has a lot to lose and doesn't want you identifying him. He really didn't have any distinguishable features?"

Atlanta shook her head tiredly. " Come to think of it, he had a purple wart on his nose and a green mohawk — I just forgot to mention it to the eleven different cops who have already taken my report."

Beck sighed, pinching the bridge of her

nose. Her head was beginning to pound. "I don't understand how you can give us so little about him."

"I'm sorry. I was a little too preoccupied with the gun pointed at my head to really memorize the exact color of his eyes." Her words were biting.

"Or you were too pissed to notice." At Atlanta's warning glance, Beck held up her hands in surrender. "Okay, I'll drop it."

Beck rubbed a rough hand across her face, dots dancing behind her eyelids. She winced at the sting it caused. She had forgotten about the mess on her face for a moment.

"For the record, you were a complete fucking idiot to go back to that car," Atlanta chided without meeting her gaze. "You could have been blown to pieces."

"I needed evidence. Something — *anything* — to lead us closer to whoever's doing this."

"You're not a detective," she muttered. "And you left me with Sid, of all people. Fucking *Sid*."

"Your mother asked me to investigate. I was following orders."

"Well, next time, follow *my* orders." Atlanta's words were cold, scathing. "Here's one for you now: go upstairs and run me a bath."

Beck rolled her eyes, sucking in a breath before she truly lost her patience — though a shred of relief blossomed in her gut at the fact that Atlanta was back to acting her usual, conceited self.

"You've got your wires crossed, love. I'm not a maid."

"You might as well have been, with all the use you were tonight." She was already pushing herself up and wandering away, hips swaying as she padded barefoot across the kitchen, with her tattered dress tangling around her ankles. "I'll run myself one, then."

"You do that." Beck stood too, ready to retire to the security office so that she could at least look into the rental company before she passed out at her desk. "G'night."

"Oh no, Miss Harris." Atlanta turned, a hand on her waist and her eyes narrowed. Punishment. This was Beck's punishment for tonight, for leaving her. She clenched her jaw in anticipation. "You can't leave. I need my bodyguard with me at all times. Didn't my mother make that clear?"

"I'm a close protection officer," Beck countered. "And I think you can manage a bath alone."

Only when she looked at Atlanta — *really* looked at her — did she catch the way her chin wobbled and the way she worried at her perfectly plump bottom lip. Her pallor hadn't returned to its usual golden glow; instead, the color had leached from her face so that she was a sickly shade of white against the smattering of brown freckles across her nose.

Afraid. She was afraid. And this was her way of telling Beck. For once, it wasn't a game.

She needed her. Had needed her, perhaps, all

night.

"Then protect me closely, Miss Harris."

With resignation, Beck closed her eyes and nodded. "After you."

* * *

"Unzip me?"

Atlanta turned off the faucet before the bubbles could brim over the bathtub. Steam rolled off the water, reminding her of the car, and of Beck, and —

No. She wouldn't keep replaying it anymore. She wouldn't feed the fear, wouldn't let it bury her. She had escaped. She was fine. She was safe. So was Beck.

Beck's calloused fingers on her back only reminded her of that. They were warm, surprisingly, and much steadier than her own. She unzipped the dress with only a lingering graze of knuckles against spine that Atlanta might not have noticed with anybody else.

"Thanks." She untangled herself from the shimmering silver until it spilled to her ankles. Beck stationed herself at the door with her back to Atlanta, hands clasped in front of her.

"Undressing in front of me twice in one day," she noted dryly. "I don't think this is in the job description, either."

"It's wasted on you anyway," Atlanta remarked, dipping her toe into the bath before she submerged the rest of her body. The water spilled across the porcelain and onto the floor tiles, but she didn't care as she sank into the foam. It was scalding enough to leave her skin feeling raw, and it unveiled her from the shock of the night just a little. She had dimmed the lights, hiding from anything too overwhelming, too bright, and all that remained was a murky glow that kept her mind subdued.

Without thinking, Atlanta plunged her head beneath the surface and counted to ten. It was an old habit her brother had taught her to keep her relaxed, calm, and it always worked. When water clogged her ears and bubbles slipped from her nostrils, there wasn't opportunity to think of much else. Her blonde hair floated in snaking tendrils above her, and she pretended for a moment that she was somewhere else. Even when she was holding her breath, though, it felt like she was drowning.

She barely made it to ten before she rose up again, gasping for breath and massaging the tender muscles in her neck. Beck hadn't moved an inch. Atlanta narrowed her eyes and pinched her nose to rid herself of the droplets before scraping off the last of her makeup with her cloth. "You were very heroic tonight, Miss Harris."

It was true: even after taking on countless action and thriller roles, and dying in most of them, Atlanta had never seen anybody as invested, determined, protective, as Beck had been tonight.

Now that she had time to recall it all without having to face imminent death, it caused something sharp to claw against her belly, her ribs.

She had never been that brave. She had never been cared for that way.

"That's not what you said earlier, Miss Stone."

"I called you an idiot," Atlanta recalled. "Most heroes are idiots, aren't they?"

"I wouldn't know," Beck murmured, low enough that her voice barely carried into the bathroom. "I'm not one of them."

"Then what are you?" Atlanta's hands curved through the water, directing it in gentle swishes across her legs and arms before she closed her eyes and rested her head against the lip of the tub.

"God knows."

"You know, you can look." She squinted one eye open, just to see if Beck took the bait. "I'm covered in bubbles anyway."

"I don't think it would be appropriate."

"Nothing about us is appropriate." It was supposed to be another jab, but it came out as a mere whisper. "Turn around, Beck."

Atlanta didn't know why it mattered so much, only that it did. She needed to see her face again, needed to know she was here. She felt vulnerable, alone, afraid, and Beck was the only person who had quelled that, tonight and at the party and in Paris, and perhaps even before. It wasn't about the fact that she was naked in the bath. It wasn't to make Beck flustered or see what reaction she might gain. She just… needed her.

And she hated herself for it. She had never needed anyone before.

Reluctantly, Beck obeyed, her shoulder pressing into the doorframe as her eyes locked on Atlanta's. They didn't stray any further down. Always so steady, so composed. Not like Atlanta The Mess. No matter how good an actress she was, and how much she joked and flirted to distract from the truth, she had never found a strength like that.

A part of her wished that she could be the one to break it in Beck, that she could affect her the way Beck did her. Only Beck hated her for being rich and famous and superficial. Atlanta would never have that power over her. She could have had any other person in the world, and yet the only one she wanted despised her. A cosmic joke. Karma, maybe, for the many mistakes she'd made in her time.

"You never asked me if I was all right."

"Excuse me?"

"After the accident. When we got home." Atlanta splashed against the water, wiggling her toes against the faucet. "You never asked if I was okay."

I was screaming for you, she wanted to say. *And you didn't give a damn about me.*

"Because I knew you were."

"Oh?" The answer surprised Atlanta, and

she raised an eyebrow. "How?"

Beck shrugged and closed the lid on the toilet seat before she sat down. Atlanta could see the tiredness pulling down her features now, etching lines at the corner of her mouth and causing her hooded lids to sag. She steepled her fingers and leaned forward. "You don't strike me as the damsel-in-distress type."

Relief lifted Atlanta. That was something, at least. Maybe Beck didn't think her weak and pathetic after all. "I'm damsel-y enough to need you, aren't I?"

Beck blinked as though trying to decipher the meaning behind her words. Paused. "Are you okay, Atlanta?"

Atlanta. Her name had always sounded so silly on everyone else's lips, but not Beck's, with the soft vowels and *T*s and the gravelly tone it was sung out with. To keep from dwelling on it, Atlanta flashed a cheap smile. "Someone tried to kill me. Twice. I'm absolutely wonderful, Beck."

Frustration tightened Beck's features, and Atlanta couldn't blame her. She had wanted her to ask, and yet couldn't bring herself to be honest when Beck finally had. It occurred to Atlanta that she still hadn't washed, so she started now by massaging her shampoo into her scalp.

"I'm sorry." The words were a sharp blade that cut through the tranquility of dripping water and things left unsaid. Atlanta faltered and lifted her gaze in surprise, brows furrowing. Beck's features were strained — the most emotion Atlanta had ever seen her wear.

"For what?"

"For not being able to keep you safer tonight."

Atlanta sat straighter, twirling her lathered hair across her shoulder. Beck's words from earlier echoed like a second heartbeat in her mind: *I couldn't protect her, Atlanta. I was too small, and we had nothing — no help, no friends, no support. That's why I am this way.* She couldn't decide whether she would rather plunge her head back into the water and never come back up for air, or get out of the tub and comfort Beck. "Beck, I didn't mean what I said before. You... you kept me as safe as you could."

"Not safe enough," she grunted, eyes straying from Atlanta's gaze. "You're right. I shouldn't have left you with Sid. My job is to stay with you. I just... I wanted to catch him."

"So that you won't have to babysit me anymore?" Her attempt to lighten the mood. She closed her eyes and sank back into the water, rinsing it free of the shampoo.

Beck let out a soft chuckle. "Well, there is that."

"You kept me as safe as you could," Atlanta repeated firmly.

Beck shot her a flat smile. "When we first met, you asked me what my real name was."

Atlanta frowned. That interaction in the

stale British bar felt so long ago now, and she couldn't imagine Beck going by anything but just that: Beck.

"It's Charlotte. Charlotte Harris."

"Charlotte." Atlanta blinked. The name had nothing attached to it: no feeling, no wanting, no curiosity. Not like Beck's. Still, the fact that she had volunteered the information.... Maybe Atlanta had been wrong before. Maybe a part of her did care. Finally Atlanta wrinkled her nose. "You're right. It doesn't suit you. Not like Beck."

Beck nodded slowly, as though she had been expecting a different reaction. Then she relaxed slightly, bracing her elbows on her thighs. A moment was shared where Atlanta was locked in place by her gaze, heart racing with want, need, and something much more overwhelming she had never truly felt before until tonight. Whatever control Atlanta had had before, Beck had well and truly broken it. This wasn't just a flirtation, a game, anymore.

Atlanta cared about her. She wanted to know everything about her. She wanted everything from her.

She bathed in silence after that, running conditioner through her knotted hair and washing her skin of any remaining dirt and blood and makeup before sighing tiredly. "Could you pass me the towel?"

Beck eyed her and then the clean white towel folded by the sink before standing and holding it out from end to end, eyes cast to the floor.

"Always so determined to protect my modesty," Atlanta muttered as she stood, dripping, and took the towel. She wrapped it around herself slowly, hoping that Beck might brave a look before she was done. She didn't, instead turning her back to her until Atlanta stepped onto the bathmat.

"Please," Beck scoffed, and Atlanta knew with just that sneer that things were back to normal between them. She didn't know if that was a good or bad thing. "I don't think you have any modesty left to protect."

"Probably not. I'm decent."

"Decently covered perhaps. Not so much as a person." Beck whipped around again, expression wiped clean of the emotion that had sullied it a moment ago. "I'll see you tomorrow, then."

The thought of being left alone caused another wave of nausea to roil in Atlanta's belly, but she couldn't beg again — wouldn't. Beck had made it clear she wasn't interested. Maybe she wasn't into girls. Maybe she wasn't into Atlanta. Either way, she tottered into her bedroom wordlessly, shutting the door against the steam once Beck emerged too, skin dewy and hair plastered to her cheeks. "Okay."

Beck hesitated, gaze lingering a moment too long while Atlanta pretended to busy herself by pulling out her slinkiest pajamas from her dresser. "Unless there was anything else."

Atlanta shrugged as nonchalantly as she

could and willed her heart to stop thundering in her chest. Anxiety must have been clear on her taut features, because Beck inched toward her.

"I can stay until your parents get home, if it'd make you feel safer."

"Are you sure that's appropriate?" *Why?* Atlanta wondered as soon as the question left her lips. Why couldn't she just tell her she wanted her here? It was as though her mouth and her brain weren't connected at all. She had spent too many years trying to separate them for the sake of her career.

"Nothing about us is appropriate," Beck echoed Atlanta's words. "But you're right. I'll go."

She made it all of three steps before Atlanta called her back. "Beck."

Beck whipped around expectantly. Atlanta took a deep breath, swallowing down the turmoil crashing around within.

"I'd like you to stay."

Beck nodded, offering the ghost of a smile. "Then I'll stay."

❊ ❊ ❊

Beck hovered in Atlanta's bedroom while she changed behind the paneled room divider, her shadow slipping through the wooded slats. Beck couldn't fathom why the actress had chosen now to stop dressing and undressing in front of her — perhaps because she had already maxed out her vulnerability for the night, or perhaps because the air between them suddenly felt ripe with something Beck couldn't identify. Electricity, sparking from her corner of the room to Atlanta's. It wasn't unusual to grow closer to a client after an incident like tonight's, but never like this. Beck's CEOs and politicians had never deigned to take a bath in front of her, that was for sure.

But Atlanta wasn't like any other client. She was wily, attention-seeking... and yet for a moment, as she had forced her eyes to remain locked on Atlanta's face, Beck had glimpsed something beneath that and wondered if it was all just a mask, like she had said on the balcony.

Beck couldn't make sense of it, so she scoured the bedroom, fingers running across surfaces free of any dust until she came to a shelf of leather-bound books. The ones Atlanta had bought in Paris were there, on the bookshelf. All classics and poetry, with a few modern crime and thriller novels interspersed between them. And then there was the typewriter on her dresser, paper flopping out of it with a few sentences already printed. Beck fought the urge to read them. Last time she had seen it, she had been certain it was unused.

She turned when she heard Atlanta's quiet feet tiptoe against carpet. "Do you write?"

The corner of Atlanta's mouth twitched with that coy smile as she pulled at the hem of her top. She wore a scanty satin camisole and lace-lined shorts in a rosy pink that set off her sun-kissed skin. Once again, Beck had to fight to keep her gaze from traveling down to her long legs. It wasn't that she was attracted to her — so she told herself, at least. It was just that anybody would be a fool not to acknowledge Atlanta Stone's beauty, and as she began to see slivers of the real woman beneath, curiosity was getting the better of her.

"Does that surprise you?"

Beck shrugged, nose prickling with the waft of smoke that still clung to her clothes from the destroyed car. She needed a shower. Desperately. "You'd like it if it did."

Atlanta narrowed her eyes and sat cross-legged on her bed, scraping back her damp hair from her shoulders. "What makes you say that?"

"You've been trying to get a reaction from me since the moment we met." There was no question or accusation there: Beck knew it to be true, and she wasn't in the habit of pretending she was an idiot.

Atlanta's eyes glittered as she watched — always watching, waiting. Waiting for what? What did she see in Beck? What did she *want* to see?

"Interesting theory." Atlanta stood, opening the first drawer on her desk and pulling out a wad of papers. She threw them down in front of Beck. The first was a title page: *"The Broken," written by Atlanta Stone*. Brows knitting together, Beck turned the page and found a script. She scanned over the words, the dialogue, the descriptions. Beck knew nothing about writing, but she could imagine this playing out on a television, could imagine herself flicking through the channels after a long day and pausing when she found this show littered among the same old sitcom reruns and David Attenborough documentaries.

"You wrote this?"

Atlanta nodded, and then winced as though remembering her whiplash. Her fingers curled around her neck, massaging the corded tendons there. "Yep."

"It's…" For once, Beck could not find the words. "Good. Have you submitted it to anybody?"

Atlanta scoffed. "God, no. They'd never take me seriously."

"Why?"

"The same reason you don't." She said it lightly as she ambled back to the bed and sat again. "Nobody does. I'm just a ditzy actress, right? My only job is to sit and look pretty."

"Atlanta," Beck murmured softly, guilt dancing in her gut, "if this is something you want, you should at least try. You're clearly talented."

Atlanta only shook her head stubbornly. "I don't think so." She sighed, shifting as though she was uncomfortable with the sudden praise. "You know, you don't have to stand over me all night. Sit."

"Am I a dog, now?" Beck retorted, but didn't argue against the invitation. She was sore, exhausted, on the brink of collapse. She shimmied her stiff arms from her now tattered blazer and draped it over the chaise longue before she collapsed onto it.

"Roll over." Atlanta's smirk grew.

"Ha," Beck deadpanned, scraping her hand across her face tiredly. "You should get some rest."

"So should you."

"Still on duty, apparently." She flashed Atlanta a wry smile to show she wasn't really complaining. What had happened tonight was bound to leave anybody shaken up. Besides, Beck was still feeling guilty for breaking protocol to investigate the SUV, even if Atlanta had — bizarrely — reassured her earlier.

"How do you make time for your personal life with a job like this?" Atlanta asked.

Beck clasped her hands together, sucking in a breath. "I don't. Then again, I could ask the same of you."

"Right." The answer didn't seem to satisfy Atlanta. "Still, doesn't it ever get tiring?"

"I like keeping busy," Beck muttered guardedly.

"So you don't have somebody waiting for you at home, then? A family, a partner, a friend?"

She shook her head, swallowing down the lump in her throat as she remembered Atlanta's harsh words. *What do you go home to when you're done here, Beck?* "I think you established that in Paris, didn't you, love?"

Atlanta wrinkled her nose. "Did I hurt your feelings, Miss Harris?"

"What am I doing in here, Atlanta?" Beck huffed, standing again and pacing restlessly. Her silk shirt slipped off one shoulder, but she made no move to adjust it. She was past caring. "What are you *really* asking me?"

"Nothing." Atlanta's voice rose in surprise as she straightened on the bed, frowning. "I'm just curious. I'd like to know who my mother hired to protect me. Is that a crime?"

"You're always playing games. Always looking for something from me. What?"

"Beck." Atlanta rose, catching Beck's wrist so that she was forced to stop. Beck wouldn't look at her. She was tired, and she'd had enough of Atlanta's torment. Enough of all of it.

Atlanta said nothing, instead stepping in front of Beck so that it wasn't so easy to avoid eye contact anymore. A muscle feathered in Beck's jaw as she swallowed, turning rigid when she finally, reluctantly, met her gaze. What she saw there took the breath from her. Atlanta, free of both her makeup and her mask. Brown eyes glistening with warmth and apology. Mouth puckered with worry. Was it real, Beck wondered, or just another game to play?

She was an actress, after all. Beck wouldn't let herself forget that.

As Atlanta dared to lean closer, their noses brushed. The almond scent of her shampoo wrapped around Beck like a ribbon, the lavender of her soap tying the knot, and her eyes fluttered shut with the comfort. Their fingers intertwined, Atlanta's soft and warm, Beck's coarse and stippled in cuts. Beck couldn't think. She couldn't do anything but breathe Atlanta in, frozen against the sudden proximity.

Until Atlanta's lips grazed hers, reawakening her.

Instinct turned Beck's posture stiff, as though Atlanta's kiss were an order roared from a stern sergeant and Beck an obedient cadet. She stepped back, swiping her clammy palms against her trousers.

Atlanta's expression twisted into pained rejection, and it sent a vicious pang of regret through Beck.

"You're here," Atlanta murmured, words so breathy they made Beck ache, "because you make me feel safe."

The house creaked and shuffled before Beck could calculate any sort of reply. A door slammed. Voices echoed. Her family was home, and Beck would have to explain what had happened to them. Wordlessly, she collected her blazer, wary of Atlanta's scrutiny as she shrugged it on quickly.

"I need to fill your mother in. If it would put you at ease, I can stand guard by your door when I'm done."

Even from the corner of her eye, Atlanta's disappointment was clear. "No," she said. "That won't be necessary. Get some rest."

"You too, Miss Stone." Beck hoped the formal address would remind Atlanta of who she was to her — and who she wasn't. What she hadn't hoped for was the flinch Atlanta made against it before she climbed back onto the bed.

"Goodnight, Miss Harris." Atlanta's dismissal was dulled, empty, hollow. Beck's chest felt bruised as she left, shutting the door carefully behind her.

She cursed herself beneath her breath with every step away from Atlanta's room.

TWELVE

Whoever the driver had been last night, he'd used an alias to rent the car. Beck had spent the better part of her morning searching through her company's database for a David Ward who looked as Atlanta had described and had been in London that night. No luck. The woman who worked for the rentals wasn't much help, either — other than supplying the fake name, she couldn't tell Beck anything of his appearance or personal details. Beck had half a mind to go down there and persuade them in person, but she didn't think it would achieve much now. The woman on the phone had said herself that they were looking for him too, what with the damage he'd caused to the car, and were having just as little luck. All Beck knew was that he had hired out the car a few hours before Beck and Atlanta had landed in LA, which meant either it was the same attacker from London who knew the Stone family's itinerary and had followed them to LA before she and Atlanta got in from Paris, or it was mere coincidence that a new attacker had popped up on the same day. The latter didn't sound very likely.

Which meant this guy wanted Atlanta

gone. Which meant Beck had to take her job more seriously than ever.

She hadn't heard from Atlanta since last night, so, giving up on her search and with Minerva's permission, she headed to the family's personal gym situated just behind the main house's garage. Filling them in last night had been difficult. Minerva had fallen into a panic as Beck explained the situation to them, even after reassuring them that Atlanta was safe and unharmed. Anderson had been, thankfully, more level-headed, and had gone to see Atlanta later on. Weston didn't seem all that fazed, but it was becoming obvious that he didn't have much of a relationship with either of Minerva's children.

Beck had lain in the dark last night, worrying she had made the wrong call, worrying about breaking professional boundaries, worrying about everything. Atlanta had gotten under her skin, and that bothered her more than anything: more than the man, or men, she was supposed to be trying to catch.

The punching bag in the middle of the gym helped. Beck drove her gloved knuckles into it over and over, numb to the aching tingle and the shallow breaths fighting to escape her lungs. Her forehead, the nape of her neck, her back, were all soaked with sweat, and still she continued, kicking and hitting with violent grunts and gasps.

"Is something working you up, Miss Harris?"

The drawl came from behind, barely audible against the blood pumping in Beck's ears. Steadying the bag, she turned to find Atlanta leaning against the cross-walker, her arms folded and a dry smirk curled on her lips. She looked much more herself than last night, though the makeup and clean, untattered sundress probably had a little to do with it.

Beck huffed and freed her sticky hands of the boxing gloves she'd borrowed. "No more than usual, Miss Stone."

As she adjusted her sports bra and leggings and pushed the flyaway hair from her face, she couldn't help but notice Atlanta's gaze lingering over her. She became suddenly aware of the rivulets of sweat trickling down her skin, and the way her stomach rippled as she wrestled for breath.

"Is there something I can help you with?"

"I just wanted to check my schedule with you," Atlanta replied. "I'm onset for a guest appearance on *Lucifer* tomorrow morning. And then on Wednesday night, I've been forced into another of Weston's charity auctions."

"And I suppose given last night's incident, I can't dissuade you from attending either of those, can I?" Beck picked up her water from the floor, nearly collapsing in the process, and gulped.

Any fear that Atlanta had let leak out of her last night was gone now. Her dark eyes were hard with determination. "I won't stop living my life because of this."

Considering her state after the gala last night, that surprised Beck. "Then I'll make sure your security is upped."

Atlanta nodded, shifting. "There was something else I wanted to ask you."

"Oh, god, what now?" Beck couldn't handle many more of Atlanta's "questions."

In response to Beck's blunt outburst, Atlanta's expression hardened. "I want you to teach me some self-defense techniques. If all else fails, I need to be able to protect myself."

"I won't fail," Beck argued tersely, putting her hands on her bare hips in disbelief. Her overworked arms burned with that movement alone.

Atlanta rolled her eyes. "Even so, I'd like to at least learn some basics. My schedule has been freed up this afternoon. I need to get changed, and then I'll meet you back here."

She was already making to go. Beck raised her eyebrows. "I didn't agree, love."

"Did I imply you had a choice?" Atlanta's question echoed around the gym's stone walls with that American lilt that Beck had, at some point, learned to accept... to enjoy, even. "My mistake."

Beck shook her head in exasperation, but by the time she had the energy to summon any sort of retort, Atlanta was gone.

Today was going to be a painstakingly long day.

* * *

"Out of curiosity," Beck rasped as she demonstrated the heel palm strike maneuver, "who else has access to your itineraries besides Minerva?"

Atlanta sighed at Beck's inability to switch off, even for a moment. She was supposed to be teaching her how to protect herself, for god's sake, but Atlanta could practically hear the cogs whirring in her brain even as she thrust out her arms. "Only my agent and personal assistant. Sometimes my publicist."

"From now on, all correspondence will have to be encrypted. He knew where you would be last night, which means he knows too much."

Nodding, Atlanta mimicked Beck's movements, slicing the air with her palm.

"Good," Beck commended. Atlanta tingled with satisfaction. It wasn't often Beck praised her for anything. "Draw back quickly and use the first opportunity to run. You can also use this movement to strike the attacker's ears. It won't do as much damage, but it will stun them enough to give you more time."

"Got it." Atlanta bit her bottom lip in concentration.

"If you're close or unsure about the strength behind your punch, use the elbow strike instead." Beck demonstrated, jutting her elbows out on either side and using them as weapons. Atlanta tried not to notice the way her muscles tautened. With only her sports bra and leggings on, her toned body was more visible than ever, stomach ridged and biceps curved. She might be only average height, but she had much more strength behind her than Atlanta would ever have realized.

Witnessing it now sent heat eddying low in Atlanta's belly, distracting her. She shook out her fingers, regaining composure before she followed Beck's movements.

"Exactly like that." Beck tightened her ponytail, tongue running across her plump bottom lip. "All right, the next one I want to show you involves more contact. If someone comes up behind you, they'll probably try to catch you in a bear hug. Do you mind?"

She had wandered behind Atlanta, her arms suspended on either side of her as she awaited permission.

"Not at all," Atlanta purred in reply, forcing down the shiver threatening to run across her spine. A moment later, Beck's arms, firm and unbreakable, were wrapped tightly around Atlanta's torso. Atlanta prayed Beck wouldn't feel the way her heart sped up until it shook her very bones.

"The first thing you should do when you're locked like this is bend forward. It's more difficult to carry someone if their weight is shifted from the center." Beck's instructions whispered through Atlanta's hair. She was so close, enveloping her in all of her warmth and support.

Atlanta did as she was told, burying her tailbone into Beck's pelvis. The contact did nothing to extinguish the flames licking through her, sparking from her very core.

She heard Beck swallow and wondered if she felt it, too, or if Atlanta was still chasing something that only she could feel.

"Now turn into me slightly." Beck's voice was unwavering, unfazed. "Send your elbows back, just like the elbow strike I just taught you, only from behind."

Atlanta did, careful not to hit Beck as she struggled out of her grip until they were face-to-face again.

"Once you've struck with your elbows, your best bet is to knee them in the groin — assuming, of course, the attacker is a man. If not, the stomach works just fine."

Atlanta drove her knee up until it brushed lightly against Beck's stomach. If she stayed this way, she could easily wrap herself around her. Instead she lowered her leg.

"At that point, I'd hunch over, and you'd be able to push me down onto the floor before making a run for it."

"Somebody else, maybe," Atlanta replied. "I think it would take a lot more to get you down."

Beck hummed, a crooked smirk gracing her lips. "Maybe. Let's try it again, a little bit faster this time."

Atlanta gulped at the thought of being touched that way again. She braced herself as Beck hooked her arms around her, clasping just below her breasts. She couldn't do it. She had to know, had to try. She sucked in a breath, melting into Beck until the nape of her tender neck was met with her shoulder. Their cheeks brushed, sending tingles dancing across Atlanta's flesh until they centered between her thighs.

"What are you doing?" Beck breathed, words a husky caress that only made Atlanta want more.

She turned, cupping Beck's jaw, and kissed her before she could talk herself out of it.

It lasted only a second. Beck pulled away, face creased in bewilderment as she kept her at arm's length with a hand against her shoulder. "What the fuck are you doing?"

"Finishing what we started last night," Atlanta replied, voice low. "I know you felt it, too. You wanted to kiss me."

Atlanta had replayed it again and again, memorizing every jolt of emotion that flashed in Beck's eyes as they had inched close enough to kiss. Beck had licked her lips, perhaps subconsciously, as though preparing them for Atlanta's. She had almost melted into her completely.

But then she had taken it all back. Called her Miss Stone. Reminded her that nothing could happen — according to her, anyway. Atlanta had never much cared for rules.

Beck's face contorted, and Atlanta felt the

change like a million splinters through her heart. "I'm not interested in being some experiment, and I certainly have no interest in risking my job for you."

An *experiment*? Atlanta took a breath, smoothed her features, put on that mask that the world loved to see. "If you kept up to date on current events, you'd know I came out as openly pansexual years ago."

Beck's upper lip curled into a sneer. "A current event is a country declaring war or a presidential election, not Atlanta Stone's choice in bedfellows. Jesus, how conceited are you?"

The condescension in those words shattered Atlanta's facade. "You think you're so much better than me, don't you?"

"I don't think anything. I *know*. I know that you spend your life concentrating on the superficial, throwing your money around while most people can't afford a fucking meal. I know that you think the world revolves around you. I know that you care more about color-coordinating your Instagram feed than actually doing something that matters."

"You don't know anything about me," Atlanta snarled, her finger jabbing the air as she took a step forward. Beck matched her by doing the same, until she could feel the anger rolling off her. "You see what you want to see. And besides, if you really thought I was that bad, why would you bother? Why not go hover around someone else? Go find some famous do-gooder who visits the children's hospital every day and takes videos of themselves feeding homeless people on the streets."

"Believe me, I'll be out of here the second you stop pissing about, getting yourself into trouble because you'd rather earn a place on the front page of a trashy magazine than protect yourself from a very real threat." Beck's accent thickened the more heated she got, until Atlanta could barely decipher the words.

"Can't wait." Atlanta spat. "Why not just save yourself the hassle and let them kill me?"

"Not a bad idea." Her nostrils flared, eyes narrowed to slits. And even now, when Atlanta hated her, hated Beck's perception of her, she still pulsed with need for her. "In fact, I should have just left you in that fucking car last night."

"You might as well have. You ran off without me anyway and nearly got yourself killed."

"To help *you*, you idiot!" Beck exclaimed, hands slapping her sides. "You're welcome, by the way."

"Right. My knight in shining armor," Atlanta seethed, taking another step forward so that Beck was driven back. And then Atlanta had backed her up against the mirror spanning the back wall, chest heaving with angry breaths and palms flat against the surface. Atlanta couldn't breathe herself, their proximity dizzying as her eyes flicked between them and their reflections. How the hell had *she* been the one to push Beck into a corner? How had it not been the other way around?

"You're fucking impossible." Beck chewed on the venom in her words, but her eyes had softened as though in resignation, and she watched Atlanta with a new, calmer focus that somehow felt more suffocating than her rage.

"You're…" Atlanta had no way to complete the sentence. Her gut was swirling with want, need, heart stuttering. "You're…"

How could Beck not feel it? How could she not sense how *badly* —

Beck's lips were on her without warning, rough and hungry and still full of fury as she kissed. Atlanta groaned into her, half in confusion and half in pleasure, as Beck's teeth skimmed her flesh and her tongue demanded access. Atlanta granted it willingly, falling apart, unraveling, melting, thawing, until her bones weren't enough to keep her upright. Her hips rolled against Beck's desperately, skin against skin, thighs against thighs. They were trying to forge together, twisting like two mangled branches of the same tree until they splintered against a hurricane.

Beck fell away first, cheeks rosy and lips swollen as she traced the phantom of Atlanta's kisses with her finger. And then her eyes widened, and Atlanta's heart sank, because she knew — even before Beck walked away, she knew. It was written all over her. Beck thought this was a mistake.

When Beck slid away from her, Atlanta fell

back and let her go. She shouldn't have watched her leave, but she couldn't look away.

And as Beck fled without looking back, Atlanta caught a glimpse of a jagged white line sitting just beside the rolling vertebrae of her spine.

A scar, stark against olive skin.

That rough, ruined flesh would be the last she saw of Beck for the rest of the day.

THIRTEEN

Beck had fucked up royally, and the only way she could think to fix it was by avoiding any conversation with Atlanta, even the next day when Sid chauffeured them to the Warner Bros. Studios together. Apparently Atlanta had the same idea, because a frosty silence crackled between them all the way there, and once they arrived, Beck stood outside her trailer while Atlanta got ready inside.

Extra security had been assigned around set today, from both the studio and the WPG. Nobody could get in or out without clearance, and they'd had another vehicle trailing them here in case the driver caught wind of their location and returned to finish the job. Atlanta had not shown a glimmer of anxiety, though she surely must have felt it after the night of the gala.

Beck did, too — only for reasons other than another potential attack.

She had kissed Atlanta. Had lost herself in her. Just for a moment, but even that was too long. She had never lost control that way before, had never done anything stupid enough to sacrifice her career — especially not for a bloody kiss with her client. *Never.*

She cleared her throat, adjusted her stance, casting a steely glower when a clean-shaven, familiarly arrogant face emerged from the trailer opposite.

Hugo Dean.

The last thing Beck wanted today was to deal with Atlanta's idiot ex-boyfriend again.

"Ah, it's the bodyguard." The twit swaggered over to Beck as pompous as ever, white teeth blinding against the midday sun. "Should I prepare myself for a brawl?"

Beck put a hand to his chest when he made to knock on Atlanta's door, nudging him back and sliding between him and his only entrance. Hugo scowled down at the contact before meeting her eyes, his own flashing with anger. She had to fight not to choke on his overpowering, musky cologne. "I don't know, Mr. Dean. Have you come to hassle my client?"

Hugo rolled his eyes and slicked his hair back, though it was already saturated and straw-like from an obscene amount of gel. "Look, I heard about the car accident. I wanted to make sure she was okay. Isn't that allowed, sweetheart?"

Beck's nose wrinkled at the pet name. She hadn't been called sweetheart since she was six years old, and even then she had thrown a tantrum to make sure it never happened again.

"She's fine." This wasn't protocol and Beck knew it. There was no reason why Hugo couldn't go in that trailer, other than the fact that he had given Atlanta unsolicited attention at the party. It wasn't Beck's call to refuse him entrance — but she wanted to, and not just because he was a first-class dick. "You'll see her on set soon."

"I'd like to talk to her now." Another false grin that probably made most women go weak in the knees. It was wasted on Beck. "Has she filed for a restraining order I don't know about?"

Beck inhaled through her nose patiently, jaw clenched tight enough that her molars scraped together. "Wait here."

She rapped on the door twice.

"Come in," Atlanta called, voice muffled on the other side of the door. Beck did, boots clanging against metal as she stepped up and let herself in.

The interior of the trailer was nothing like Beck had expected. Atlanta had her own en suite, bed, couch, television, kitchen, and god only knew what else in here. She could have lived in here for months at a time, let alone a day. In fact, she probably had more luxuries under this tiny roof than Beck's family had ever possessed in her childhood home. Atlanta sat by the vanity, reflected face illuminated by a circle of white bulbs while a makeup artist hovered over her, powdering her cheeks and painting her lips.

Lips that had pressed so forcefully into Beck's yesterday.

She realized too late that she was standing at the threshold with her mouth agape like an idiot. "Hugo Dean is outside, Miss Stone," she said hastily to shatter the silence she had dragged through the door with her. "Should I send him in?"

To Beck's relief, Atlanta let out a long sigh. "I suppose. Keep your gun handy, though... Miss Harris." The name was added as an afterthought, as though she had forgotten for a moment that things were uncomfortable and they could no longer engage in their usual little quips.

"Don't tempt me." Beck opened the door and motioned for Hugo to enter. He did, having to duck his head to fit into the small space. His tall frame eclipsed Beck's as though she were no longer there.

She could have left. She should have been stationed outside, as she was before. Instead she remained by the door, clawing at her collar when it stuck to her skin. Stuffy. It was stuffy in here, despite the air-conditioning humming from a vent in the corner.

"Hey, Lanta," Hugo greeted. Apparently, his limited vocabulary could not manage three syllable words.

Beck choked down her sneer, sniffing instead. Her nose burned with a strange scent: subtle, but sulphurous. It didn't sit right with her, and the back of her neck prickled as she examined the trailer through narrowed eyes. "Has somebody been cooking?"

"What?" Atlanta frowned, dismissing her makeup artist with the wave of her hand. She swiveled in her chair to face both Beck and Hugo, hair bouncing in tight curls around her face. "No.

Why?"

"It smells off in here."

"Anyway," Hugo interjected. "I heard about the accident —"

"I noticed that earlier, too. I thought maybe somebody had used my en suite and forgotten air freshener." Atlanta seemed not to pay any heed to Hugo either. She stood up, tucking her dressing gown across her torso as she followed Beck into the kitchen, though she was clothed underneath in the same casual jeans and tee Beck had seen her in this morning.

Nothing seemed amiss, the surfaces all clean and no damp bubbling beneath the wallpaper.

There was not much else in here. Nothing but a cluster of white, wilted roses on the kitchen counter.

"How long have these been here?" Beck was already pulling out her gun, not that she could use it if what she suspected was right. A gas leak. Beck would wager that it wasn't a coincidence Atlanta had been stationed in the stuffy, smelly, flower-killing trailer.

"I delivered them this morning, just before you got here," Hugo answered. "How the hell did you kill 'em so qu—"

He hadn't the chance to get out the question properly. Beck cut him off, urging Atlanta out. Her stomach churned with the sense of imminent danger, much like the dread she had felt pour through her in her military days. "Everybody out. Now. It's a gas leak."

They didn't need to be told twice. Beck kept Atlanta's body guarded with her own as they scrambled out, the makeup artist and Hugo leading in front. She didn't care where they went after that. She was already guiding Atlanta to the nearest point of safety: Atlanta's car, parked in the lot beside the trailers.

Beck only noticed now that Atlanta had emerged barefoot, and it slowed them down a little as Beck screamed for everyone loitering around to move, go. If the thing blew —

No sooner had she begun to dread it than it happened, a bone-rattling explosion reverberating through the asphalt, into their bones. Beck shielded Atlanta from the soaring debris without a moment's pause, forcing her blonde head down as a burst of black, billowing smoke and bright orange flame bled into the clear midday sky, turning it murky. For a moment, there was no Beck, no Atlanta, only war, bombs, death. She lifted her head and felt as though she were back, tethered by a helmet and a machine gun and a scratchy, uncomfortable uniform.

But she wasn't. The fog of old memories cleared and made way for new ones. Instead of dust, she choked on fire. Instead of a rifle, she gripped her revolver. She kept it poised, ready if anybody used the explosion as an opportunity to ambush them, but the place had erupted into screeching chaos. An LA officer whose name she hadn't bothered to remember ordered Beck to evacuate through her earpiece — as if she needed to be told. She lifted the cuff of her jacket to her mouth and spoke through her own radio. "Stone is with me, unharmed. Get a car ready."

"Already done, Harris. Head toward the studio parking lot."

Beck stood, looping her arm through Atlanta's and running, sprinting, to the black car idling by the curb. The screaming crowd around didn't deter her, nor did the deafening shriek of an alarm whining from somewhere nearby. There was pandemonium, shrouding them like flashing lights on all sides, and at its core, its heart, there was Beck, guiding Atlanta unwaveringly, legs burning and teeth gritted.

She wouldn't let them touch her. She wouldn't let go of her.

Atlanta's breaths fell in uneven rasps as they weaved through bedlam, through bodies, through cars, to the parking lot. Despite the rough ground matched with no shoes or socks, she didn't falter, didn't slow them down.

When they reached the car after what felt like an eternity, Beck checked through the window to glimpse the driver. She had to be sure they were getting in the right car. It was Carson who sat behind the glass, gripping the steering wheel with one gloved hand and urging them in with another. Atlanta collapsed onto the leather seats and grappled to haul Beck in with her before Beck could look back. She barely had time to close the door before they were rolling out of the lot, away from the studio and the flames and the mayhem.

"Put your seatbelt on," she demanded of Atlanta. "Are you hurt?"

Atlanta shook her head as she obeyed, face pale but otherwise unblemished. "No, no, I'm okay. How the hell did you know?"

Beck didn't have an answer. She put her gun away and only then caught sight of the familiar gray eyes staring at her through the rearview mirror. "I didn't even know you were here, Michael."

"I was reassigned last minute," he replied, fingers thrumming against the wheel. After days of only hearing from Americans — other than Eric and occasionally Phil in the office — Carson's eloquent London accent was a blessing to Beck's ears. "Good job, too."

Beck nodded and sank back, eyes scouring Atlanta once more to double-check for injuries — only to find her frozen, bone-white, her gaze fixed on Carson. Her fingers trembled as she took her phone from the pocket of her robe. Trust the actress to get ahold of that before bloody shoes.

"Are you sure you're okay, love?" The *love* slipped out before she could stop it, but she was no longer thinking about how she should have addressed her. Her only instinct was to fight, to protect, and if Atlanta was not okay, neither was Beck.

Atlanta typed something into the notes app on her phone, tilting her screen toward Beck. "I'm fine. Just shaken up."

That wasn't what the text read, though. The words printed in bold, unmistakable letters sent a sickening pang of dread through Beck.

It's him.

* * *

Atlanta's heart felt as though it might tear itself straight from her chest — either that, or jump out of her throat and onto the black leather seats of the car.

Beck knew him. She *knew* him. She had gotten into the car thinking that they were safe with him. *How?*

Atlanta was still half-deafened from the blast in the trailer, and she could smell the fire on her clothes, on her skin, in her hair. It had taken everything in her to type those two words on her phone and show Beck, uncertain that Beck would understand or believe her.

She shouldn't have doubted her.

She realized that when Beck scanned the words and her expression turned grave. Her throat bobbed with an aggressive swallow as she lifted her gaze to the man in the driver's seat — that short-haired, graying, brawny man who had held a gun to her head not all that long ago. It was him. His features, though difficult to distinguish in any other setting, were unmistakable now. He was dressed in a professional suit, rather than the plain black hoodie and loose jeans he had worn to steal from her family, to shoot her stepfather, to threaten her.

Was he one of them? Did he work with Beck?

His eyes locked on Atlanta's in the rearview mirror, gray and piercing and life-altering, and she knew she was right. It was him. And they were in the back seat of his car, being taken god knew where.

He had planned it all. He had known to have a backup plan. He wouldn't let Atlanta go again.

She wanted to vomit.

Instead she searched Beck desperately. Her olive skin had paled to a sickly gray, lips down-turned as she examined the words and then Carson again.

"How long have you been in LA, Michael?" Beck questioned with perfect nonchalance, as though she were just making small talk. *A better actor than me*, Atlanta thought, and fought to mirror that mask. Unless she wasn't acting. Maybe she didn't believe her. Maybe Atlanta had mistaken that look of realization a moment ago. "It wasn't so long ago I saw you in London."

"I got in last Thursday." His voice was gruff, accent much more clipped than Beck's: the type of British Atlanta was used to faking for roles, rather than the soft lilt she had become accustomed to over the weeks.

"Thursday," Beck repeated. The day before they had flown in from Paris. Beck's hands were crawling to the holster beneath her jacket. She pulled something from it, slipped it slowly, quietly, to Atlanta.

Atlanta took it with unsteady fingers, keeping one eye on Carson as she slid it into her own jeans, beneath the dressing gown she'd never had the chance to take off. God, she was going to die barefoot in a fluffy Warner Bros.–supplied robe.

"Yep." Carson nodded.

When the cold metal bit into Atlanta's palm, she knew what it was that Beck had given her: a gun. It was small — probably the pistol she had lent out to Sid the night of the crash — but that was probably for the better. She could hide it this way, and he wouldn't expect her to be armed, either.

"Are you sure?" Beck mouthed as Carson began to flick through radio stations, white noise spasming gradually into an obnoxiously upbeat Harry Styles song that did nothing to quell Atlanta's nerves.

Atlanta nodded determinedly, eyes blazing. *Yes. Yes, it's him. Please, Beck. Please believe me.*

Aloud, Beck said, "Who were you assigned to this time?"

"Oh, just the usual. A reality star with a stalker. Nothing came of it, so they thought it better to use me where I was needed after the situation here worsened." His eyes found Atlanta's again in the mirror. Her expression remained tight, steady. She wouldn't let him ruin her, no matter how badly she feared him. "Apologies, Miss

Stone. I didn't properly introduce myself."

"No need." Atlanta's voice was hoarse and not her own, but she pasted a small smile across her lips. "The two of you have worked together before?"

"Michael worked with the company long before I did." Beck's brows were furrowed. Atlanta could no longer see her face: she was staring out of her window at the high California hills and burnished soil — calculating, maybe, hopefully, how the hell they were going to get out of this. Atlanta squinted into the bright sun and, glimpsing road signs for Sun Valley, saw that they weren't headed back into the center of LA, but away from it. "We've been assigned to the same clients a few times. Work in the same office a lot."

Finally Beck picked up the phone that Atlanta had left unlocked between them and typed before passing it back to Atlanta:

When I tell you to run, you run.

Atlanta had to bite down on her tongue to keep from protesting. The thought of moving, running... she didn't know if she could. Beck, though, remained steadfast, eyes glittering with stubborn commitment.

She would have to.

Beck's hands fell to Atlanta's slowly, and she squeezed once as though in plea. *Please.*

Atlanta nodded. It was all Beck needed. She unclipped her seatbelt silently and reached for the revolver in the holster by her other hip. Then she unfastened Atlanta's, too.

Beck shimmied into the center, carefully, while Atlanta shifted closer to the door. Without a trace of reluctance, Beck dug the barrel of the gun into Carson's temple. It gave a sickening click as she turned off the safety, index finger snaking across the trigger.

"Pull over, Michael. Now."

Atlanta had come across some terrible actors in her time. That was why, when Carson gasped, hands dropping from the steering wheel for a moment and the car swerving just so, Atlanta could see right through his pretence. "Jesus, Beck, what the fuck?"

"I won't ask again," Beck warned, words cut from steel. "I don't want to hurt you, but I will. Pull over."

They were veering off from the main road and headed uphill, toward the infinite mountains rolling out ahead of them, scorched a dry redbrown by sun and scattered with brushwood.

"Beck," Atlanta whispered desperately, panic thickening her words. He couldn't take them any further. Picket fences and the flash of other cars were becoming sparser the higher they got. They'd be in the middle of nowhere soon, with nowhere to run.

She'd been holding her breath, and she realized it only when Carson glanced up again.

Any doubts Atlanta had dissipated when he smiled — that same twisting, sick grin that he had cast her that night in London, drawing his cheeks up into lines of stubbled flesh. And then he dragged the steering wheel to one side all at once, tires screeching against concrete as they turned. Without her seatbelt, Atlanta fell into Beck. Gun forgotten, her arms circled Atlanta protectively, both a shield and a tether — until they plummeted, the car an insignificant stone careening downhill, windows shattering with bones and engine screeching with their own screams.

They were suspended there for a lifetime, and then all at once, they weren't.

All at once, they weren't anything at all.

FOURTEEN

All Beck knew was dust and agony. She coughed up grain, throat burning, before she even opened her eyes. Warmth trickled across the side of her face, past the seam of her lips, until she winced against the coppery taste and finally found the energy to prize apart her lids.

The world was upside down... but she wasn't. She lay against fragments of glass that pinched her flesh in all places, Atlanta a deadweight on top of her — but awake. Stirring, at least. Her blonde hair tickled Beck's nose as she groaned. Carson remained in the front seat, head brushing the ceiling and body suspended by his seatbelt. Unconscious. Trapped.

Beck checked her ears: her earpiece was still in, and somebody was screaming at her down it. Eric, it sounded like, though she had no idea what he was saying. His voice crackled and broke.

She drew her arm up slowly and spoke into her radio. "This is Officer Beck Harris. Atlanta Stone is still in my protection." She winced as something, somewhere, twinged in pain, her voice hoarse and brittle. "We were taken hostage by Michael Carson. We crashed just off the La Tuna

Canyon Trail. I need backup here immediately."

The only response was more broken words. Beck had no idea if they'd heard her. It didn't matter, though: Atlanta was trying to get up now, panicked breaths escaping her as she clutched the passenger seat.

"Are you okay?" Beck groaned, relieved when Atlanta hauled her weight off Beck so that she was no longer pressed into the glass.

"I think so," Atlanta whispered.

Beck sat up slowly and gauged her next move. Their best bet was to climb out of the rear window, but that would mean smashing it. "I need to put this window through so we can get out. Shield your eyes."

Atlanta nodded, wide-eyed as her gaze finally flitted to Beck — and froze there. "Oh my god, Beck."

"It's okay," Beck breathed, clutching her ribs as she readied herself. Dizzying pain washed over her, and she gritted her teeth until it passed. "Just do as I say, and I promise I'll get you out of here."

"You're hurt."

"I'm fine," she countered, sounding more confident than she felt. "Now do it, please."

Atlanta hesitated before nodding and turning from the window. Beck sucked in a breath, counting to three before she kicked her boot through the window. The glass rained down on them. Beck hid her face in her hands until it was safe, and found when she lifted her gaze back up that there was enough room, now, to escape.

"Now I need you to climb out for me. Carefully as you can."

"What about you?" Atlanta questioned.

"I'm right behind you, promise."

Atlanta nodded, shimmying over the seats until she reached the rear window. She clutched the frame until her hands were bloodied by broken glass and crawled out, debris crunching beneath her legs. Beck followed at a much slower pace, sharp shards sinking into her flesh until her fingers buried into hard, hot, grainy soil and she was freed. Atlanta helped her stand, and Beck kept her knees stiff to fight her teetering balance.

"Have you still got your gun?"

Atlanta shed herself from her grubby robe and clutched the pistol still tucked in her jeans. Her face was tainted by black dust, but she seemed otherwise unharmed. Beck could release a breath, at least, for that. "Yes."

Beck pulled out her own revolver and made sure it was loaded as she glanced behind her at the wreckage. It was... well, she didn't know how either of them had survived it. Smoke rolled from both sides of the car, metal skeleton crushed and scraped and torn. They had fallen from quite a height, but she could glimpse the road still in view above them. No cars had yet passed.

No one had seen them.

It felt wrong to still be enveloped in unsullied blue sky, vast and endless and blinding. The heat beat down on Beck and she wondered again if she might collapse.

Beck cursed upon noticing Atlanta's bare feet, already torn and bloody. "Can you walk?"

"Yes." Atlanta frowned, hand cupping Beck's cheek suddenly. She could still feel that hot stickiness crawling across her skin, matting her hair and pooling in the collar of her shirt. "But, Beck, you're bleeding."

"It doesn't matter." Beck swallowed, fingers curling around Atlanta's for just a moment before she searched her pockets. She swore again when she saw that her phone had been another victim of the crash. It came out of her jeans destroyed. "Your phone. Where is it?"

Atlanta tucked her hands into her pockets desperately, tears filling her eyes. Her entire body trembled, and a lump rose in Beck's own throat at the sight. She hadn't been able to protect her. Again. She had failed her. Again.

She had let this happen.

Unwilling to show Atlanta her weakness, she turned and wiped her grimy face with her sleeve — and froze.

Carson was hauling himself out of the car, a hunched, broken figure covered in glinting glass. Instinct threw Beck in front of Atlanta, and she pointed her revolver at him. Lips pursed, Carson lifted his gaze and pointed his own gun at her. His tie hung askew around his neck, top button undone and blazer torn. Both a friend and a stranger.

It didn't make sense — and yet it did. Why hadn't Beck questioned him at the hotel that day? How hadn't she realized? She had worked with this man for years, and yet he bore another face now. The face that Atlanta had described him, had had him drawn up by a sketch artist, and she still had not thought anything of Carson. He matched the image perfectly, all gray and cold.

She had been right, though: he didn't have any distinguishable features. He resembled any other athletic, middle-aged Londoner with light stubble and closely shaven hair. That was why he had been so good at hiding. He was the perfect criminal, with a perfectly forgettable face.

"Don't move," Beck ordered, eyes narrowing to slits as she took a step forward. "It's over, Michael. Whatever you're doing, it's over."

Carson didn't stop. He pulled himself up by the lip of the car until he stood in front of them, gun extended. Beck's fingers quivered on the trigger.

Could she do it? Could she shoot a man she had worked side by side with for years? They had laughed together, talked together, kept one another company on exhausting assignments. He had told Beck about his wife and his daughter, his life.

Sucking in a breath, she steadied her shaking hand. If it meant protecting Atlanta, whom she could feel so close behind her now, she would.

"I mean it, Michael. Stop where you are."

His mouth twitched with the beginnings of another chilling smile, but with a ragged gasp, he held his hands up and let the gun fall to the dirt. "Look at you. Protecting *her*." His voice was gruff, dull eyes hard as stone. "You used to mock her kind in the office. Now you're her little lapdog."

"As opposed to a criminal?" Beck retorted, slanting her head as she scrutinized him. "God, what are you doing, Michael? Why?"

"*Why*?" he repeated incredulously. His face contorted, wicked and bitter. "They were in possession of a necklace — *one* fucking necklace, Beck — that was worth enough to buy half of London. And for what? For an auction, where another rich twat could throw their money at it until they get bored of it, too?"

"That necklace was for a charity auction," Atlanta interjected shakily. "The buyer's money funded starving children and helped build new schools in developing countries."

Carson scoffed, a venomous, cutting sound. "Is that what they tell you, princess?"

Beck felt Atlanta stiffen. "Share with the class."

"Weston Wilder is a conman. That donation doesn't go to charity. It all goes back into his bank account. Do you think all of that money he splashes on you comes from the sky, love?" He was asking Atlanta, peering around Beck. A ferocious, hot anger bubbled in Beck's veins at the way he spoke to her, the way he called her "love" as though it could mar everything she and Beck had shared with that same stupid name.

"He's my stepfather. I have nothing to do with his money." Atlanta's voice wobbled as she stepped forward, until she was beside Beck. Beck cast her a warning glare. Though Carson was seemingly unarmed now, Beck didn't trust him — not with Atlanta. She needed her safe. "I don't even go to his auctions half the time. God, I don't even *like* him. Why come after me?"

"You saw my face. You knew too much." Carson cast her a disdain-laced grimace.

It occurred to Beck then that he was being honest: too honest. This man had used aliases and had threatened to kill to keep his secret. He had planned the perfect way to get the two of them alone today. Why give up now?

Unless he didn't think it was over. Unless he thought he still held the power and could get out of this scot-free.

Stepping forward to cover Atlanta, Beck scanned him again. His eyes were made of ice. Madness didn't swim in them, not yet, but something else did, something cruel and determined. "So what would *you* have done with the necklace, Michael? What makes you any different from Wilder?"

"Our job is to take frauds like him down."

"*Our*?"

He faltered. She had caught him out.

There were more of them. An organization

or a syndicate, probably, just as she'd guessed.

"Who's 'our,' Michael?" Beck questioned. "Robin Hood and your Band of Merry Men? Who do you work with?"

"It isn't too late to join in, you know." He lowered his hands slightly, and Beck pointed her gun with more force. There was no fear in him, though. Maybe she had been wrong about him: maybe he was just a fool. "I know how much you hate them, too. You could stop them, Beck. You could stop all of it."

"That's awfully kind of you, but I think I'll pass." Another step toward him. His fingers twitched against his palms, and she knew. He was planning something. He hadn't surrendered yet — wouldn't, probably, until he had gotten what he'd come here for. "Atlanta, go."

"No," she croaked behind Beck. Beck drew her eyes from Carson long enough to scowl at her.

"I need you to find help. Go."

"*No*," Atlanta repeated with more force this time.

"You already have me where you want me, don't you, Beck?" Mischief glinted in Carson's eyes. "What difference does it make now?"

A shudder skipped down her spine, turning her cold. He moved quickly enough that she hadn't the time to shout for Atlanta to move. One moment his arms were up, elbows out, the next a blade was in his hand.

He flung it at the same moment Beck threw

herself at him, intercepting his aim as they rolled into the dust. The dagger clattered against rock somewhere distant. She should have shot him when she'd had the chance, but she couldn't. He had a daughter, a life. How, then, had he sacrificed everything for this?

His weight on top of her stole the breath from her lungs, the gun snatched from her hands in a second. He straddled her with the cool barrel pointed to her head. She didn't balk, didn't flinch, only stared blankly up at the man she had once thought a friend.

And then, as his finger curled on the trigger, a click from above. Atlanta's frame blocked out the scorching afternoon sun and cast Beck's world in shadow. The pistol Beck had given to her was pressed into the back of Carson's skull, her beautiful face hewn from cool marble.

"I wouldn't, if I were you."

He didn't listen. Instead he flailed his arms, knocking the pistol from Atlanta's grip before his other arm whacked her to the ground completely, tumbling away from Beck. The whimper that left her sent a jolt of aching fury through Beck.

Atlanta still found strength enough to fight back, kneeing him in the groin as he went to pummel her again, just as Beck had taught her. Reeling, Beck hauled herself upright as Atlanta fought to escape, their groans mingling as she knocked the revolver from his hand and ran.

Ran, through fumes and dirt and debris,

golden hair whipping behind her.

Carson unfolded from the ground with the revolver, held the gun up, pointed it at her.

A final, overwhelming rush of adrenaline ricocheted from Beck's toes to the crown of her head as she stood. Atlanta wasn't running away, but running toward her. She would have cursed at her over and over if she'd had the time.

But she didn't. Carson's finger returned to the trigger. Beck sprang toward him and bent his arm back with a revolting crack. They both collapsed with the bone-chilling peal of gunshots, a searing, splintering pain tearing through Beck as she fell with him, metal digging into her shoulder.

It didn't keep her from aiming the pistol Atlanta had dropped straight into his chest and shooting.

Carson clutched his chest, blood blossoming from the breast pocket of his white shirt as he fell limp on top of her. Beck whimpered and rolled his motionless body away, glad when his face was turned into the dirt so that she could no longer see the evil, dying husk of the man she had once thought a friend.

Agony punctured through her shoulder, guilt through her soul, and she did not know which one to clutch first. She went for her arm, fingers slipping against thick blood. Atlanta stood over her a second later, blonde hair haloing her heart-shaped face, tears gleaming pearls in her eyes.

"You idiot," she cried as sank to her knees, replacing Beck's hands with her own. She pressed down ferociously on the wound to quell the blood flow. "You stupid, stupid idiot."

Despite her pain, Beck bared her teeth into a strained grin. "You're one to talk, love."

"Shut up," Atlanta snapped. The fingers of her free hand curled into Beck's shirt as though trying to keep her here, with her. Beck wanted nothing more.

She coughed out a laugh and clutched Atlanta's blood-speckled hand tightly, relief flooding through her at the sound of sirens wailing in the distance. It was over. She cast a glance back to Carson to make sure of it, ice burying itself into her stomach at what she found. He hadn't moved. He was gone.

Beck had killed him.

"You shouldn't have done that," Atlanta whispered, tilting Beck's face back to her. *Her*. Her cheeks were smattered with dirt and tears and blood, but she was still beautiful. The worry, though... the worry contorting that face was enough to make Beck's heart plummet down, down, down.

"It's my job," Beck murmured as Atlanta applied pressure to her wound again. She interlaced their fingers with her other hand, worrying at her lip as she looked anywhere but at the blood, the mess. Beck clung to consciousness only for her, squeezing so tightly she could feel Atlanta's bones crunching.

"I think you need a new job." Atlanta shook her head and pressed her lips to the back of Beck's grubby hand. So soft, so lingering. It only reminded her of how it had felt to kiss her, and she held on to that while glimpses of blue and green figures trampled down the hill in the corner of Beck's blurred vision. She blinked, swallowed, ached.

"At least those self-defense lessons came in handy."

Atlanta let out a mangled laugh, brushing Beck's hair from her face. It was true, though. Atlanta had taken care of herself today as much as Beck had. She looked up at her now, wreathed in blue sky, and saw so much more than she had when they'd first met. She was strong, defiant, unbreakable.

She was hers.

She was glad when Atlanta finally kissed her. Though Beck's lips were chapped and bloody and full of dust, it didn't matter.

Only she mattered. That, and the fact that she was safe. The pain burrowing in her flesh and bones was secondary to that.

She was safe. Beck carried that comfort with her into the darkness.

FIFTEEN

Atlanta couldn't bring herself to move. Not until Beck could. She waited, waited, waited, for what felt like hours, days, with her hand in hers, covered in grime and blood and memories she couldn't rid herself of. Facing death again. Escaping it again. Being pushed far from its jaws by Beck.

She had taken a bullet for her. The evidence was on the bloodied bandages wrapped around Beck's shoulder, poking out of the thin bedsheets.

It was the quietest Beck had ever been, and the most peaceful, too. Her features were smooth, soft, in unconsciousness, her face younger when it wasn't creased with worry or frustration or pain.

When had Atlanta fallen for that face? When had she let herself care so much that sitting here, thinking of Beck's body crashing to the ground in the wake of a bullet, made her heart crumble so agonizingly that she had to shut her eyes against the pain?

She still saw it behind her lids. Still heard the gunshots.

When she opened them again, Beck was gazing at her, eyes glassy and lids drooping from the morphine they had pumped into her. A breath of relief fell from Atlanta. Her eyes welled with tears as she leaned forward in her chair and brushed Beck's matted, bloody hair from her cheek.

"Idiot," she muttered again for good measure. She never wanted to feel so cold, so afraid, so without Beck again, and this was the only way she could think to tell her.

Beck's lips puckered with a smile, but it soon fell. She dragged her head up from the pillows, face creasing in pain. Atlanta stood alert, pushing Beck's good shoulder gently back to the mattress.

"What are you doing? Lie down."

"I have work to do. Carson." Her words were barely coherent, thick with agony and painkillers and the lingering dregs of sleep.

"Lie down," Atlanta hissed. Of course Beck paid her no heed, instead pushing her back as she swung her legs round slowly until they dangled from the bed. "Carson is dead."

Beck blanched, gripping her arm. Finally she stopped moving — but Atlanta wasn't glad anymore. Not from the way her lip trembled. "I killed him."

"He would have killed us both," Atlanta whispered weakly, intertwining their fingers again. It was as though Beck couldn't see her, couldn't feel her, anymore. She was somewhere else, eyes gazing unseeingly at the X-rays pinned to the screen and the IV drip by her side. "You did what you had to do."

Beck's face hardened all at once, as though remembering who she was, who she was supposed to be. The mask no longer fooled Atlanta, though. It was good, yes, perhaps even better than the ones she donned herself, but it wasn't enough. Atlanta knew who Beck Harris was now.

She knew the ache that must have been clawing through her chest, because Atlanta felt it, too.

"What about Weston?"

"I told the police everything. I told them what Carson said." Atlanta had never liked Weston. She'd felt no obligation to protect him, not if it was true that he had gotten her into this mess — and she wouldn't put it past him. It would hurt her mother, yes, but Minerva could handle herself. She would have to.

"And?"

"And they've informed the FBI. They're going to investigate."

It seemed to put Beck at ease, because she nodded and slumped slightly, knuckles burying themselves into the mattress. "Are the rest of your family safe?"

"Yes," Atlanta assured her. "They've upped security at the house, and the FBI are checking that nobody else at your company was involved with Carson's organization. Everything is taken care of, Beck."

Beck inhaled raggedly, examining the gauze

on her shoulder with more than a little distaste. "I suppose I'm no use to you like this, anyway."

"Yeah, well, as soon as you're out of here, remind me to fire you for jumping in front of a damn gun."

She let out a low chuckle that sent relief curling down Atlanta's spine. "You're welcome, love."

"It's not a joke," Atlanta spat, but her hands found the bare knee of Beck's unwounded leg and squeezed. "You shouldn't have done it. I could have dodged it."

Beck rolled her eyes. "This isn't one of your action movies. And I was doing my job."

"You could have *died*."

"So could you." It was an accusation, but Atlanta knew the blame did not lie with her. Atlanta recognized that guilt dancing in Beck's eyes from the last time Atlanta had almost gotten hurt. Beck was criticizing herself, hating herself. It seemed that nothing she did felt enough for her. A hero through and through. "I should have known. I should have figured it out. I saw Michael in the Langham before we went to Paris, sniffing around, and I didn't bloody well think —"

"He was your friend." Atlanta swallowed the lump in her throat. "You couldn't have known, Beck."

"I *should* have," Beck bit back.

Atlanta shook her head, cupping Beck's face in her hands. God, all she wanted was to fend off all of that guilt, that pain, that she now understood to be residue from a childhood spent fighting, protecting, suffering. "You saved my life. You did everything you could. Don't you dare *ever* think that's not enough."

Beck loosed a strained breath, letting her forehead fall to Atlanta's. They stayed that way as she blinked away her tears, jaw clenching against Atlanta's fingers. For the first time, Atlanta did not feel the steadfast strength of her; for the first time, it was she who had to keep Beck together, who had to stop her from destroying herself.

It made her wonder how Beck had done this for so many years.

"I was terrified of losing you." The terror had been plaguing Atlanta for hours, until she was no longer afraid to admit it. Beck had to know what she meant to Atlanta, whether she felt the same or not.

"Have you been checked out?" Beck pulled away just far enough to trace her fingers across the now cleaned bruises and stitches dotting Atlanta's hairline and cheeks. The tube in the back of her hand followed, pulled taut on the edge of the bed. "Are you okay?"

Atlanta suppressed a scoff. Of course Beck cared more about Atlanta's well-being than her own. "I'm fine. Promise. You saved me, Beck Harris."

"Always will."

Their lips were so close. The IV drip and

blood-pressure monitor behind Beck blurred into nothing, until there was only her, tangling her hands in Atlanta's knotted hair and trying to keep herself together. Beck leaned closer, eyes fluttering shut as their noses brushed.

The kiss wasn't desperate, as it had been the other times. It was slow, careful, tender. They weren't angry or afraid anymore. They were just them, and Atlanta was grateful that they were both alive to see this moment at all.

She tasted of smoke and salt and copper, a reminder of what they had endured together.

A reminder of what they had survived together.

Beck didn't pull back, and it was the only confirmation Atlanta needed. It was not one-sided. It had never been one-sided. Somehow, despite their differences, they had fallen into one another completely.

Atlanta never wanted to be torn away from Beck again.

SIXTEEN

The WPG's LA headquarters were stuffy and un-glamorous, with walls made of glass where the sunlight flooded in and cubicles separating each desk from the next. Beck limped past and was glad that the workers could not stare at her in plain sight, at least. The doctor had ordered her to rest and provided her with a sling, but she had left it in her office at the Stones' today. Her shoulder was healing fine.

Atlanta had scolded her for it, of course, but if she thought that Beck was about to start taking orders now that they were... well, kissing a lot and arguing less, the actress had another thing coming. Nothing between them had been spoken about or labeled yet. They had tumbled into a chasm together and decided not to emerge. They just *were*, for now, content in their own little patch of shadows. After almost losing Atlanta, almost losing *herself*, and with Minerva's reluctant blessing since Beck was no longer officially working for the Stones, Beck was okay with that. In fact, she was more than okay with it, even if the actress was still a beautiful pain in her arse.

Beck rapped on the glass door of the head

of security loud enough to break the silence of the office and waited. Heidi Webb, LA's head of department, motioned her in with the beckoning of her finger from behind a perfectly organized desk. Somebody else had already made themselves comfortable in the chair across from her. Another had been pulled out for Beck, and she collapsed into it without awaiting invitation as her shoulder began its habitual midday throb.

"Miss Webb." Beck nodded finally. "I'm close protection officer Beck Harris."

"Oh, we know who you are." Webb grinned with a flash of brilliant white teeth, silky black bob rippling as she nodded in awe. Beck shifted uncomfortably and glanced at the other woman sitting beside her. "This is Joanne Roth. She works for the FBI."

Beck frowned and mumbled out a "Pleasure to meet you."

"Likewise," Joanne replied, crossing one leg over the other to display the badge clipped to her belt. She sat stiff-backed in her chair, eyes sliding over Beck with clear scrutiny. "Miss Harris, I had Heidi call you in today after reviewing your work on the Michael Carson case."

"I didn't really work on the case," Beck replied carefully, shaking her knee nervously. "More just protected my client from imminent death."

"Nevertheless, we were quite impressed. You really stuck your neck out, and it wouldn't be the first time. You have quite the history of successful assignments. I saw in your records that you were in the military before you were hired by WPG."

"I was." Beck was about two seconds from running straight out of the office. She wasn't one who could handle praise simply for doing her job. Besides, she had realized a little bit too late that something more than just her career had motivated the protection of Atlanta. It felt wrong to be rewarded for all of the protocols and rules she had broken. "Sorry, but I'm still not sure why you're here — or why I'm here, for that matter."

"We're here, Miss Harris" — Joanne let out a dramatic sigh, crossing her hands at her knee — "because Carson was only the beginning of this crime ring. There have been strings of armed robberies and attacks on some of the wealthiest people in the world, and we're certain that they're all connected."

Our job is to take frauds like him down. Carson had confirmed there were more of them. This wasn't news to Beck. She nodded to signal her knowledge, teeth sinking into her bottom lip. "They think themselves vigilantes, I think. Said they were taking down frauds like Weston."

Joanne nodded. "Only a lot of the people involved are innocents, such as your client, Miss Stone. They're just as criminal as the people they target, and just as fraudulent. We need agents skilled enough to handle a case like this. Miss Harris, we need *you.*"

The words settled in silence, resonating against the glass walls like metal prongs whistling out after being struck against the table. "Me?" Beck repeated, jabbing a finger into her sternum incredulously. "With all due respect, Miss Roth, I'm practically a glorified babysitter."

"It can feel that way, can't it?" Laughter fringed Joanne's words as she shared a glance with Heidi. "But the truth is, there are not that many people willing to protect others. You've proven countless times that you're willing not only to stand guard, Beck, but to fight. You're tough. You get the job done. Frankly, I want you on my side."

It didn't make any sense. The guilt she still felt each time she saw Atlanta's healing wounds. The fact that she had not figured out sooner that Carson had been behind it. And she had killed him. "My client was injured in the altercation, and I was close friends with the perpetrator. I... I don't think I'm the hero you think I am."

"I think that your striving for perfection only proves to us that you won't let us down." Joanne reached out, putting a hand on the arm of Beck's chair. "You did a wonderful job, Miss Harris. Don't doubt that. You don't have to make a decision now, but think about it."

Beck could barely signal her agreement in her daze. Joanne stood, Heidi escorting her out, and then it was just the two of them.

"Can I ask you something, Beck?" Heidi questioned as she sauntered back to her desk and perched on the edge. She was relatively young to be so high up in the company — not like her boss back in London, who was a decaying, bald man that Beck had never really trusted. No, Heidi's features were only a little bit wrinkled at the edges. She was probably only a decade older than Beck, at most.

"Ask away." Beck tilted further back into the padding of her chair, preparing herself for the worst.

"When you took the bullet, did you think about it beforehand? Did you hesitate?"

Lines creased Beck's forehead as she pondered the question, remembering that hellish day and the fear that had come with it. Carson had pointed the gun at Atlanta. Beck had known that if she didn't move then and there, he would hit her. She wouldn't have been able to live with that. She'd never let a client die on her watch, least of all Atlanta.

Even before that, putting herself in harm's way for the sake of someone else had come second nature. She had been doing it for about as long as she could remember. It wasn't something she'd ever had to think about, not since the first time she had seen her mother suffer. It was instinct — and that instinct had intensified threefold with Atlanta in the line of fire.

"No," she decided finally. "No, I didn't think or hesitate. I just acted. I knew I had to do it. That doesn't necessarily mean I'd be able to bring down a syndicate, though."

"Maybe not." Heidi shrugged, dark eyes glittering. "But wouldn't it be fun to try?"

Beck let herself grin at that, her attention sliding down to her heavily padded shoulder. It would be fun. It would also be dangerous.

But it had always been dangerous for Beck. That had never stopped her before.

So what was stopping her now?

*　*　*

Atlanta neatened the thick pile of paper on her dresser as Beck entered her room. She had long since stopped knocking. Since she was on sick leave until her shoulder healed and Minerva didn't technically need her aid anymore, all professionality had gone out the window. Minerva had been certain at first that Atlanta was teasing when she had told her about her feelings for Beck, but Beck's constant, lingering presence beside Atlanta had convinced her these past weeks that they were more serious than Atlanta's usual flings and one-night stands. Since Beck had practically saved Atlanta's life and Minerva was forever indebted to her because of it, she had let it slip more easily than expected.

They hadn't really spoken about what it all meant themselves. They had been too busy giving statements and dealing with Weston to focus on much else. He had been arrested not long after Beck had come home, and Minerva had posted his bail before kicking him out of the house when she found out about his stolen money stowed away in a separate bank account. It had been a messy, stressful fortnight, and Atlanta couldn't have gotten through any of it without Beck: the nightmares, the memories, the arguments, the echoes of Carson and gunfire.

It was difficult to remember that she was safe now. Easier, though, when Beck came through the door.

Atlanta greeted her with a wide smile, taking special care to draw her attention to the manuscript beside her typewriter.

Beck frowned in suspicion as she collapsed onto the bed. "What?"

"Oh, nothing." Atlanta fiddled with the corner of her title page before gathering the pile and throwing it down beside Beck. The papers rippled, held together with two rings punched through the margin.

Beck unlaced her boots before she gathered the manuscript and scanned over it. "It's your screenplay."

"Yes, it is."

"Either you're very excited about binder rings, or you're trying to tell me something."

"Well." Atlanta pulled a brown envelope from the sheets and slipped the manuscript in before sitting. "I decided that I'm going to send it to a few directors I've worked with. See what they have to say."

Beck's hazel eyes brightened, cheeks rounding with a proud smile that sent an aching warmth through Atlanta's veins. God, nobody had ever looked at her like that before, as though they thought she was capable of anything. It made her feel like perhaps she was. It made her feel less like the mess she had gotten so used to being. Finally, she was shedding her skin and stepping into a new one entirely.

With Beck.

"That's amazing, Atlanta. They're going to love it."

Atlanta answered her words with a soul-crushing, heart-wrenching kiss. Everything in her tingled with Beck. Her soul breathed for her, breathed for the way she softened only for Atlanta, and the way that somehow, after everything, she still saw something worthwhile in her.

They fell onto the mattress, Atlanta careful not to press her weight onto Beck's arm as she straddled her and slipped her tongue past the seam of Beck's soft lips.

"Jesus," Beck breathed between kisses. "Have you missed me, love?"

Atlanta answered with a mangled, moaning hum, her fingers finding the hem of Beck's shirt. She slipped it over Beck's head gently, one arm at a time, before her mouth grazed across the crook of her neck, where the smell of her leathery perfume was strongest. Atlanta could have stayed tangled this way with her for hours. Beck had been so reluctant at first to start this with her. Now she bunched Atlanta's dress up her thighs, strong hand gripping her hips until Atlanta ground herself into her.

Fingers crawling across Beck's neck, to her shoulder blades, Atlanta felt the mound of scarred tissue beside her spine and stopped. She drew away only slightly, her hair curtaining both of their faces. "What happened, Beck?" she whispered cautiously. She hadn't dared to ask before now. "The scar on your back. What happened?"

"I was…" Beck licked her lips and swallowed against the hoarseness coating her throat. "I was caught in a stabbing when I was sixteen. Where I grew up…" A wry smirk. "Well, it wasn't exactly Beverly Hills."

Atlanta's brows knitted together. *Sixteen.* She was just a kid. It killed Atlanta to think of Beck suffering that way. "Did they catch the person who did it?"

Beck shook her head, eyes glazing over as Atlanta sat up. All heat between them had been stifled for now, lost to the intensity of the conversation. Atlanta preferred it that way, though. She yearned to know every piece of Beck, no matter how painful. "I'm sorry."

Beck shrugged, wincing immediately in regret, and propped herself against the headboard. Her right shoulder was only covered in a small dressing now, the wound almost healed. Another scar to add to the collection; this time, because of

Atlanta. "Could've been worse."

"It shouldn't have been." Atlanta grazed Beck's chin with her thumb delicately. "What was the meeting about?"

In a moment, Beck's expression shuttered back to that usual guardedness that Atlanta had so hated once upon a time. It came and went, pushing Atlanta in and out of Beck's life when it pleased. A sturdy wall Atlanta was determined to overcome. "Nothing interesting."

"Tell me," Atlanta pried, locking her fingers with Beck's: her way of keeping her here, with Atlanta. She was so afraid that any moment, the dream would be shattered and Beck would be ripped from her. She had been with so many people before, but never anybody like this. How long could she keep Beck? Beck, who would never be fully hers because she was not used to giving away parts of herself. Beck, who restrained herself in everything she did, keeping a constant veil between herself and the world. Beck, who hated so many things about Atlanta's lifestyle.

They were so different. Atlanta was always waiting for Beck to remember that and run straight out of the door. And yet she hadn't, yet. A part of Atlanta still hoped she never would.

Beck swallowed and sank back into the pillows, dark hair splayed out across satin as she looked up, past Atlanta, to the ceiling fan. "I was offered a job."

Atlanta frowned. "You have a job."

"Not by WPG." Beck worried at her lip, fidgeting restlessly. "By the FBI."

Ice pooled in Atlanta's gut. Perhaps she should have been happy, supportive. Instead, she could only think of what that could mean. If Beck wasn't a bodyguard anymore, she had no reason to stick around. She had no reason to stay. "Oh. What kind of job?"

"They think Carson was part of a much larger organization. They want me to help them put an end to it. They want me as an agent."

Despite her fear, pride swelled in Atlanta. Of course they did. How could they not? Atlanta could imagine her now, stopping more people like Carson from hurting anybody else. "What did you say?"

"They told me to take some time to think about it." Beck sighed, playing with Atlanta's freshly manicured nails absently. "I mean, it's a silly idea. I didn't do anything extraordinary."

"The only person who really believes that is you," Atlanta scolded, brushing a stray piece of hair from Beck's eyes. "I don't think the FBI would offer just anyone a job. They clearly believe you can do this."

A deep hum, as though she was unwilling to admit that Atlanta was right. "I don't know."

"What's holding you back?" A selfish part of Atlanta wanted Beck to say "you," but she knew better. Loving Beck was accepting that the only thing that ever truly held her back was herself.

"I don't know," she repeated. "What if I'm not right for it? I made so many mistakes with you."

Atlanta's heart twinged. Was *she* a mistake? "Mistakes?"

"I didn't keep you as safe as I should have." The relief at that was so strong that Atlanta's ribcage almost collapsed.

"We've been over this." Atlanta rolled her eyes and began carving circles into Beck's thigh. "You wanna know what I think?"

"You *think*?" Beck retorted, an echo of how they had once communicated. "I didn't know you were capable of it."

Atlanta knew the taunt meant that she was deflecting and ignored her. "I think that you've spent so long protecting other people that you're afraid to let it go. You've spent your life trying to make up for what happened to you as a child." Beck winced at that. "Being an agent would mean taking a step back from the people you protect. It wouldn't just be fighting or guarding anymore. That scares you. But, Beck, you'd still be saving people. You'd still be doing what you do best. You'd still be you."

"So you think I should take it?" Beck murmured.

"If it would make you happy." Atlanta shrugged and planted a kiss in her hair. "Would it?"

"You were right with what you said in Paris.

I spend my life on my feet, trying to fill this void I've always had… and then I go home to nobody. I worry that if I keep this up, if I take this job, I never will."

"Well, stop worrying," Atlanta said, as though it was simple. "Make the world a little bit safer, Beck. And then come home to me."

Beck blinked, stunned. And then she pulled her head off the pillow, propping up on her elbow, to find Atlanta's lips. Atlanta wanted nothing more than to ask her to stay. Beck had become the center of Atlanta's universe. She had found herself searching for that anchoring presence these past weeks wherever she went, felt off kilter if she wasn't near. In a world that never stopped moving, Beck had become Atlanta's salvation, her shield. She had come to rely on her too much.

But she would let her go, now. The rest of the world needed Beck just as much as she did, and she was trying something new: she was trying to stop being so selfish, so self-absorbed, so self-obsessed.

She was trying to become self-reliant. Independent. And she would. But she would also cling onto Beck with both hands until it was time for goodbyes.

So Atlanta drank up every bit of Beck Harris she could get while she still could. The world would have to wait for now.

EPILOGUE

Three gunshots fired. The bullets all sank into one hole directly in the center of the target, and Beck grinned with pride as she lifted her goggles and holstered her gun. Joanne, her new boss, patted her praise on Beck's shoulder as she admired her handiwork. "Remind me never to get on your bad side."

"Oh, don't worry. I know you wouldn't dare." Beck slipped her helmet off, sighing in contentment. It had been a strange change, joining the FBI, but one that she had come to enjoy much more than working as private security detail. Though she hadn't found any more members of Carson's organization yet, she grew closer every day.

She would bring them down. That much she was certain of.

She left her gun in her locker and shrugged herself out of her bulletproof vest before collecting her jacket and phone. *Home.* Despite her love for the new job, she couldn't wait to go home.

When LA had become home, she didn't know. After she recovered from her injury, she had found a studio apartment to rent not too far from Beverly Hills, which put her at equal distance between work and Atlanta. Atlanta had offered to pay for a fancy penthouse instead, of course, but Beck liked the smallness of the one she rented now. It made her feel as though she hadn't strayed too far from who she had been in London, even when everything else had changed.

The sun lowered between the Hollywood hills as she drove home, parking in the small garage beneath her complex before heading inside. She caught a whiff of Atlanta's floral Chanel perfume before she had even made it up the stairs, and couldn't fight the smile that rose to her lips. Things were good between them despite all of their differences. It shouldn't have worked after the way it had started... but somehow, it just did. Beck had long since stopped questioning it.

That wasn't to say they didn't bicker like they used to every now and again. They were the people they'd always been; not even love could change that.

The overpowering, stinging reek of burning greeted Beck as she stepped into her apartment. She placed her bag on the floor, a cacophony of clattering pots and pans singing a welcome as Atlanta danced around the kitchen in a golden patch of fading light. Beck shook her head and sidled up to her, arms winding around her waist and stopping Atlanta in her tracks. "I thought I told you not to use my kitchen, Miss Stone," she muttered against Atlanta's back.

"Oh, stop it." Atlanta sank into Beck as she

stirred a grim gray sauce bubbling on the stove. Beck's brand-new countertops were scattered with grated cheese and smeared with butter, slivers of spaghetti littering the place from floor to ceiling. "I'm trying to do something nice for my girlfriend."

"Cooking for me is the opposite of nice, love." Despite her quip, Beck's stomach warmed, and she had to pry herself away from Atlanta to sit at the breakfast bar. Two bottles of champagne had been stationed in an ice bucket there.

"What made you think I was talking about you?" Atlanta brought the wooden spoon to her mouth and licked gingerly at the sauce she'd been tending to.

Beck rolled her eyes and pulled out one of the bottles, eyeing the brand. She didn't know much about champagne, since she had never been able to afford anything but the cheapest bottle of prosecco in her local Bargain Booze, but she had a feeling this was worth more money than everything in her apartment. "What's the occasion?"

"I'm glad you ask—"

"Hang on." Beck coughed into the back of her hand. "Before you tell me, please save whatever poor thing you are currently charring in my oven."

"Oh, crap," Atlanta cursed, slipping on a pair of oven mitts before she bent to open the oven. Thick smoke billowed out of it, curling around Atlanta.

"Jesus." Beck came to life quickly, grabbing a

tea towel and wafting the smoke detector so that it wouldn't start screeching, thus inevitably pissing off every one of her new neighbors. "You know, I was craving charcoal, too."

Atlanta shot a glare over her shoulder as she pulled out a tray of black lumps, still coughing. What type of food they had been before Atlanta had gotten her hands on them, Beck couldn't tell. Still, no matter how she teased, Beck was proud of her. Atlanta had finally begun to stand on her own two feet — or totter on them, at least, but she would steady herself eventually.

"I think I'll order a pizza." Atlanta pouted over her latest victim, wiping her hair from her face with her mitts.

"Well, the fire department didn't come out this time." Beck finally thought it safe to stop wafting, and sat back down at the counter. "I'd call that a win."

"At least we have champagne. And I brought dessert." Atlanta stood on her tiptoes to collect two glasses from the cupboard — Beck refused to own anything as fancy as champagne flutes — and placed them in front of her. Despite the commotion of a ruined dinner, Atlanta's wide grin remained unwavering as she peeled the golden foil from the lip of the bottle.

Beck raised an eyebrow curiously. "Are we celebrating?"

"I'm glad you ask," Atlanta mimicked her words from earlier, grimacing as she popped the champagne open. The foam brimmed from the neck, across Atlanta's fingers. She licked the fizz from them quickly before pouring their drinks. "I received a very interesting phone call today from Angela Harewood."

"Ah." Beck feigned understanding, though she had no idea who Angela Harewood was.

"She read my script." Atlanta's brown eyes lightened, dimples framing her smile.

Beck straightened with sudden realization. A director. "And?"

"And she wants to make the show. She's going to discuss next steps with me next week!"

"Oh my god," Beck exclaimed jaggedly, rounding the counter to gather Atlanta in a bone-crushing hug. "That's amazing, Atlanta. It really is. I'm so happy for you."

"I couldn't have done it without you," Atlanta whispered, drawing away. Beck didn't waste the opportunity, peppering a quick kiss on her nose as her fingers tangled into Atlanta's blonde hair.

"Nonsense," Beck chided gently. "This was all you. I'm proud of you, love."

Atlanta's cheeks flushed with a timidity she showed rarely. "Beck."

Beck hummed in question, her touch dancing down the nape of Atlanta's neck. The champagne and burnt food were long forgotten now. It was just the two of them. It had always been just the two of them.

Atlanta sighed, bracing her forehead against Beck's. "I know it's probably too soon, but... I love you."

Panic. It was what Beck expected to feel. It never came, though, masked by the relentless fluttering in her belly. Because she felt the same. Somehow, Atlanta had become the very thing Beck had never known she'd needed. Before her, she was always fighting, always surviving. Now, she lived. Everything she had lost as a child had come back to her at once.

She wouldn't let it go again.

It wouldn't be easy. They would always clash, but they would also slot together in the strangest and most unexpected of ways. And they would grow.

Together, they would grow.

Beck tugged Atlanta closer still, until no space remained between them. They were strongest like this, when they were knotted into one being. "I love you, too," she breathed.

Beck couldn't remember the last time those words had left her lips, but she knew she wouldn't come to regret them.

They were true. She kissed Atlanta wrapped in the absolute certainty that what she had said was true.

ABOUT THE AUTHOR

Rachel Bowdler is a UK-based graduate of English and creative writing who spends most of her time away with the faeries. When she is not putting off writing by scrolling through Twitter and binge-watching TV shows, you can find her walking her dog, taking photographs, and reading fantasy novels.

PRAISE FOR AUTHOR

The action had me on the edge of my seat. I absolutely loved this novella and can't wait to see what the author does next!

I wanted something entertaining, gripping and quick to listen to. This novella was exactly what I was looking for.

A pleasant surprise.

BOOKS IN THIS SERIES

Romancing the Stones
Celebrities and siblings, Atlanta and Anderson Stone, find themselves dragged into the darkest sides of Hollywood when their safety is compromised in two gripping standalone romantic suspense novellas.

Saving The Star

Hollywood actress Atlanta Stone has always been regarded as a vain, out-of-control party girl, and she's more than happy to play that part. However, when she's assigned a bodyguard after surviving a near-fatal robbery, she finds herself chafing against the sudden loss of her independence — the damsel-in-distress role has never been her style.

And close protection officer Beck Harris isn't too fond of her new charge, either. As a bodyguard to celebrities, Beck has spent years perfecting her cool composure around the rich and famous, but when forced to handle a wily, superficial actress intent on pushing her boundaries, her professionalism is pushed to its limits.

Their clashing lifestyles and temperaments take a back seat when a string of attacks on Atlanta suggests that she has become more than a victim of a botched robbery — now she's a target, and if Beck can't figure out who's behind it, they'll never get the chance to see who they are behind the masks they've perfected.

The Secret Weapon

When his best friend, Roxanne Wilde, is murdered and he is the last to see her alive, Hollywood heartthrob Anderson Stone is snatched from his comfortable life of wealth and fame. Riddled with grief, he is determined to seek the truth behind her death — and when bold FBI agent Jade Sawyer makes him an offer he can't refuse, he just might get the chance.

But upon embarking on an undercover operation where Jade and Anderson must pretend to be a couple, Anderson soon finds out that there's more to Roxanne's demise than meets the eye. A secret underground society of Hollywood elites named the Dawn has been festering through LA for decades, rife with debauchery and criminal activity that just about everyone he knows seems to be involved in.

As they waltz their way into VIP rooms and exclusive masquerade balls, Jade and Anderson begin to uncover the truth behind everyone's favourite stars.

BOOKS BY THIS AUTHOR

A Taste Of Christmas

Safe And Sound

Dance With Me

The Fate Of Us

A Haunting At Hartwell Hall

Handmade With Love

Partners In Crime

Paint Me Yours

No Love Lost

Holding On To Bluebell Lodge

Along For The Ride

The Divide

The Flower Shop On Prinsengracht